MONQUHITTER
SUNDAY   SCHOOL

PRESENTED TO

Sandra Mackie

FOR

PERFECT
ATTENDANCE

THE HARVEYS SEE IT THROUGH

THE HARVEYS SEE IT THROUGH

_by_

PHYLLIS GEGAN

COLLINS
LONDON AND GLASGOW

This Impression 1969

CONTENTS

CHAPTER ONE

THE FIVE HARVEYS

MIRANDA LOOKED up lazily into the apple tree from the swinging garden seat. The metal framework was rusted and rather rickety; the pattern on the padded seat and cushions had lost its hard, bright colouring long ago, and had now settled for an amiable blur of soft yellow, orange and green.

As she pushed one foot against the ground to make the seat swing slightly she noticed that one of the cushions was beginning to ooze its grey flock filling. " Middle-age-spread," she murmured. " I must mend it. How I *hate* sewing up seams that have split; they're bound to go again before long."

One leg, with its disreputable old tennis shoe hanging by one toe, swung gently in time to the seat. She looked around at the garden, its grass nearly the colour of hay, and worn into patches. " We really ought to do something about it," she said for the hundredth time, but she felt that there was not much chance of that yet.

The garden was almost square : nearly the length of a tennis court and slightly wider. The four of them practised tennis on it, with a length of chicken wire for a net. When the boys wanted to play cricket the wire came away, and soon, a well-worn track showed where the runs had been taken.

There were supposed to be flower-borders down each

side but balls—tennis, cricket, and even football and netball in the winter, discouraged all but the most tenacious of plants. At the far end, Miranda had sown lettuce and radish seed and had raised mounds for cucumbers and marrow. She had great ideas of saving on the housekeeping money and had erected a barricade of planks, boxes and more chicken wire to defend her seedlings from balls, brothers and cats.

It was Friday, the first week of the long holidays. " Nearly eight weeks for the four of us," she thought, " and then G.C.E. for me next year . . . Dad will be home early to-day—I ought to go in and start on the potatoes. I wonder if Verna has thought to lay the table. Why *did* Mrs. Bostock have to break her leg just before we broke up, poor thing ? "

The Harveys—Dad and the four children—had had a succession of housekeepers since Mrs. Harvey had died, which was when Giles, the youngest, was a year old. Miranda had been seven at the time, and Julian and Verna came in between. For the last year they had managed without a housekeeper, Mrs. Bostock from the village coming in for five mornings a week.

Miranda got herself regretfully out of the seat, went in, and got potatoes ready for chips. Verna soon sauntered in and made a long job of laying the table, for she would stop and gossip about everything that was going on.

" Get *on*, Verna," Miranda exclaimed. " And take the end of your left-hand plait out of the lard."

" Ugh ! " Verna wiped the end of it with a duster. " Aren't the boys in yet ? "

" Don't think so. Julian is doing caddie for old Major Morris, to earn an honest penny, and Giles might be anywhere. Oh—here they are. I hope aged parent won't be long." Miranda was reading Dickens and was liable to quote him at any time.

But their father was late that evening, not early. The fish was keeping hot in the oven, and beginning to look like dried-up plastic, Verna moaned, while the boys were reduced by hunger to eating bits of bread broken off the loaf.

When he did arrive, and they had all started to eat, Mr. Harvey told the family what had delayed him.

"The firm is sending me over to America and Canada for a few weeks. Business is beginning to expand a bit, after being in the doldrums for some time. We've still got to go cautiously, but Big Boss thinks that we might try for some overseas contracts, and thinks that it'll be worth the expense."

"America! Canada! Oh—lucky *you*!"

"When will you be going, Dad?"

"On Tuesday. It's short notice, but I'm going to the big Trade Fair in New York while I'm there. Now—do you think you can manage on your own for six weeks?"

"Of course we can. Manage on our heads. Bring me back the top story of the Empire State Building. They'd never miss it."

There was a lull for a moment while the boys collected the plates up, and Miranda fetched the stewed apples and custard, made that morning. Their father cast a slightly harassed look around.

"Now, you've got enough clothes for the six weeks, haven't you? One on, one off, and one in the wash?"

"Not three caps, I haven't. And I've never tried sending my one cap to the wash."

" *Very* funny, I don't think ! " Julian felt bound to keep Giles in his place, because he thought his young brother was too precocious for a nine-year old. Giles never intended to be cheeky but words fascinated him, and whatever was in his mind had to come bubbling out.

" That'll do, you two. Miranda—send the sheets to the laundry, and you can take the rest to the Launderette. And surely you can give that ghastly ironing a miss ! "

" Wear rough-dried clothes I will not," Miranda said decidedly. " I'll do the drip-dry things at home, and Verna and I will iron the Launderette things."

" Oh, and another thing," their father said. " You'll be on your own during the day, but I don't hold with your being alone in the house at night. No," he added, as there was a burst of protests," it's just an idiosyncrasy of mine. And you can look that one up in the dictionary, Giles ! I've been dashing round, and I've heard of a woman secretary who's got to change her digs. I've offered her the top room free for the six weeks and the use of the gas-ring on the landing, if she'll sleep in. So that's that. Her name's Miss Hodges."

" She won't have to bring us up, will she, while you're away ? " Giles had none too pleasant memories of some of the housekeepers.

" No, Giles. I don't expect you to give her any trouble, and I'm sure she won't be any bother to you."

" What shall we do if anyone's ill ? " Julian suddenly realised that he would be the man of the house, in a way.

" Well, for goodness' sake ! You're not nitwits : you can cope with most emergencies. Get the doctor, or at a pinch, send a wire to my Aunt Eleanor. Can you two girls do something about that top bedroom ? Is there enough spare bedding ? "

" Just about. But we'll have to bung in all the hot-water bottles we've got. That bed hasn't been slept in for ages and you can get rheumatic fever if you sleep in a damp bed, and then we'd probably be liable." Miranda did not want complications to arise while her father was away.

" Then that's all right. Oh—I forgot. I asked her to come to tea to-morrow so that you can get acquainted. Get something in, will you ?"

" Grub, or light refreshments, Dad ? "

" Humm . . . refreshments, I should think." " Grub " was what they had when their friends came : sticky buns, and crab paste, and honey, and rather gooey cakes which oozed mock cream or jam whenever you took a bite ; for anyone who had to be treated more formally, there were " refreshments "—sandwiches, which the girls hated cutting—and things like macaroons and shortbread which the boys looked upon as elegant rather than filling.

Miranda and Verna spent most of Saturday morning going over their father's clothes. Miranda gave her sister the jobs suited to an eleven-year old, such as sewing on buttons, but she herself nobly undertook the turning of a shirt cuff which was rather worn.

" I hope she won't want to *marry* Dad, like that Mrs. Wilson did," Verna remarked, as they humped over the mattress up in the top bedroom.

" She'll hardly see anything of him, and we can get her out of the place directly he gets back. If she's found rooms, that is. We must keep on the lookout for any."

There was a rather subdued atmosphere at tea-time.

Mr. Harvey had "basely deserted" his family, as Julian put it, and would not be in till later.

Miss Hodges had fairish fuzzy hair, rimless glasses and rather a prim look. Miranda felt rather awkward at the head of the table pouring out the tea, and trying to catch Julian's eye when the visitor's plate was empty.

"I believe you had a housekeeper until recently," Miss Hodges remarked.

"We've had swarms of them," Verna said cheerfully. "Well, six, I should think—good, bad and indifferent. The last one wouldn't get up in the mornings, and she sold our remaining silver spoons."

"Yes, and then last year, when I was fourteen," Miranda went on, "my father said that if I could manage with a woman from the village five mornings a week, and everyone doing a bit, he thought we'd all be happier. He said that after all, some girls in the East are *married* at fourteen, and have a house *and* a husband to look after."

"It's a big responsibility for you—Amanda, is it? I can't remember your names and ages."

"It's Miranda. Verna's eleven, and then there's Julian, he's thirteen, and Giles is nine. I'm fifteen."

"Rather outlandish names," Miss Hodges commented frankly. "My parents thought Ethel good enough for me."

"Our parents gave us unusual names in the hope that we might find them useful in after life—if any of us wrote bestsellers, for instance, or acted at the Shakespeare Memorial Theatre——" Julian explained.

"Dad said that they thought of calling me Sam Otis K. Harvey," Giles announced, "because with a name like that it's almost impossible not to be in big business, and they thought one of us at least might keep them in comfort in their old age. But I think he was joking, really."

Miss Hodges looked at them all as if she couldn't quite make them out. " It seems a bit casual to me," she remarked, " your father going off like that and leaving you with a complete stranger. It doesn't seem to worry him. Bit happy-go-lucky, seems to me."

" Oh, but he's not like that really," Verna said in a shocked voice. " He takes a lot of trouble over bringing us up. He says that it's mostly done by trial and error, but that he thinks we haven't turned out too badly. He found out that you were perfectly respectable—— " Miss Hodges looked up with a startled air, for she had never thought to question this. ——" He wouldn't have let you come if you hadn't been."

" And he knows your employer, Mr. Banford. And he said that Mr. Banford spoke highly of you."

Miss Hodges seemed slightly reassured. " Well, I only hope that you can cope with everything, then ! I'll be getting my own breakfast on the gas-ring, and a hot drink at night, but I'll get my meals out. I'll keep my room swept and dusted too, but I shan't feel like cooking for anyone after a hard day . . . "

" We shall manage quite well, Miss Hodges," Miranda said in her most grown-up voice.

" She's quite good at managing, really," Giles declared. " She's quite good at a lot of things, like turning sheets to the middle, which I think is quite a clever invention. She's going to take her G.E.C. next summer."

" That's General Electric Company," Julian said scathingly. " I've told you that before. It's G.C.E."

Giles felt that they were getting away from the subject.

"You needn't think that Dad doesn't bother about us, Miss Hodges," he said earnestly, for he had a strong sense of loyalty. "He never calls us darling or lovey-dovey, or anything soppy like that, but he's just as fond of us as any father. It's just his way."

They were all rather relieved when tea was over and they were standing politely on the doorstep to see her down the path.

As the two girls turned into the hall Verna said, "I don't think Dad is likely to want to marry anyone who holds her knife like a pen and is called Ethel."

"We can't talk about her like that when she's just eaten our salt," Miranda said reprovingly. "And it'll be more difficult when she's here. You're not supposed to criticise visitors while they are under your roof."

"She must have some good points," Verna said philosophically.

On the Monday evening Mr. Harvey gave last-minute instructions.

"Now don't eat out of tins, will you? Only one tin of anything to be opened a day, that's an order. Plenty of fresh fruit and veg."

"Can we have cream with fruit sometimes, Dad? We get lashings of custard at school dinners, all of us, and we're sick of it." Julian spoke for them all.

"Well look—I'm giving you six weeks' housekeeping money, Miranda, in six envelopes. If you're extravagant one week, and live on lobster and asparagus and chicken and peaches you'll have to balance it the next week with herrings, and stewed apples from the garden. Or rather, apples from the garden which you will stew, to be more

precise. So you needn't look at me like that, Giles ! . . .
And you must jolly well make the money last, Miranda.
It'll be good practice, and as good, if not better, than a
term at L.S.E. for you."

" The London School of Economics," Julian murmured.

" Julian, you can see that all doors and windows are
locked at night. Verna, you do the shopping from
Miranda's lists, and Giles can run the vacuum cleaner
over the carpets. Oh, and the pocket money ; Julian,
you give it out, and no advances unless there's a really
good reason ! Miranda has the last word in any dispute.

" One last thing—I'm leaving this five pounds for
emergencies. I'll fix it with sel otape to the back of the
Saint Christopher picture in the hall, and I'll trust Saint
Christopher to look after the household. And if I give
out any more money I'll have to hitch-hike to the boat."

CHAPTER TWO

FOUR ON THEIR OWN

On Tuesday morning Mr. Harvey went off. A friend from down the road had offered to drive him to the station in the family car—a vehicle which was fast becoming eligible for the old crocks' race—and would then drive it back to Garrick Road. The good-byes were to be said at home, because all the family disliked waiting about on railway platforms and trying to make bright, casual conversation.

Mr. Grant was to come at a quarter to nine, and as zero hour approached, Miranda found the lump in her throat increasingly difficult to swallow. Verna kept blinking what she would not admit to be tears out of her eyes, while the boys had the forlorn look of dogs whose master is leaving them behind.

" Have you got everything, Dad ? "

" Do you think you ought to take a clothes brush ? "

" No—I've got absolutely everything I need, even a penknife with a gadget to take stones out of horses' hoofs. Is that the door-bell ? "

" Yes. Giles has gone. I'll take the big case out, Dad, if you'll bring the zip-bag."

While Mr. Grant was putting the luggage in the back of the car, Mr. Harvey came back to say good-bye.

" When we've gone, put on the radio," he said. " There's some pop music on the Light." He looked at them all for a moment as if he was going to give them last minute instructions, but then gave them all a quick hug and dashed out.

" Good-bye ! " he called from the car. " Look after yourselves, and see that you're all in one piece, each of you, when I come back."

" I *hate* good-byes ! " Miranda said, as they turned back into the kitchen where the uncleared breakfast table, with its plates coated in congealed bacon fat, made her feel rather sick.

" Switch on the radio, will you Giles ? " she said. " Let's stack the washing-up on the draining board for now, Verna, and we'll do it in half an hour."

" I'm going to mark off the days until Dad comes back on the calendar." Julian jumped up and got the " country cottage with roses round the door " calendar from the sitting room and drew a red ink line all round the next six weeks. " I'll cross off each day when I lock up at night."

The lively music was cheering them up and soon they were all whistling, humming or grunting, according to talent, more or less in time to the tune.

" What's this ? " Miranda suddenly said, feeling a wad of something in her blazer pocket. " Oh yes— it's the six envelopes with the housekeeping money in them."

" Pity we haven't a safe to keep it in," remarked Julian.

" I asked Dad whether I should keep it under the mattress, but he said that's the first place burglars look, so we decided on a good place. Giles, you know that spike thing we keep the old grocery bills and receipts on, that's hanging on the inside of the pantry door ? Get it, will you ? " Giles brought the spike, which had a wooden base with a length of wire sticking up from the middle and curved over so as to hang on a hook.

" I keep meaning to throw away a lot of the oldest bills," Miranda said, " but it's a good thing I didn't. I'm going to spike the envelopes near the bottom—nobody would be likely to look among old household bills for money." She took out a pound note for the house-keeping purse, then slipped the envelopes on the spike and covered them with a batch of old bills. " There ! " she exclaimed. " No one would know that this stands between us and starvation."

" And don't anyone go tidying it away into the dust-bin," Julian added. " I don't fancy living off the hedge-rows. I should think you'd get awfully tired of wild berries and crab apples and nuts."

" Did Dad remember to put the five pound note behind Saint Christopher ? " Giles asked, as they finished the washing up.

" He's sure to have. Let's go and see." They trooped into the hall and Julian got down the picture of the Saint carrying the Holy Child, and turned it over. There, neatly fixed down with sellotape was a new five pound note. " I vote we keep that intact, if we possibly can," Julian said. " Show we can be businesslike. Live within our income."

Something was pushed through the letterbox and fell with a plop on to the floor.

" I know this writing," Verna exclaimed, picking up the letter. " It's for you, Miranda, from Mrs. Bostock, I'm sure."

"I hope her leg is going on well," Miranda remarked, opening the letter. "It's addressed from Lindford, so she's at her sister's. She was going by ambulance."

"She loves writing letters," Verna told them, as they went into the kitchen again. "Did you know she has a pen friend in Huddersfield? A mother with five children and eight grandchildren. She got her through that weekly rag she buys, 'Mother's Friend.'"

"I bet they write and tell each other how many teeth their latest grandchildren have, and about wearing wool next to skin," Giles said. "She's always talking about that."

"She's rather a pet," Miranda said, smiling, when she had read the letter. "I must write to her."

"What does she say?"

"I'll read it to you."

"Dear Miss,

I thought I would just drop you a line dear hoping that you are managing on your own. Seeing has I cannot come to oblige for three months at least dear, but the Dr. says he thinks my leg is doing nicely. There are some bits of old vests in a carrier bag under the stairs dear which will polish up the furniture beautiful but do not use to much of that new polish, I always say you cant beat elbow grease altho some people who go out to oblige ladies do not seem to know what that means. The window cleaner is due round any day now, not a penny more than seven shillings for the lot and daylight robbery but they all ask the same dear, not like when I was first married half a crown and glad to get it.

Must buzz off now dear as whats your line is on in a minute or two. So bye bye for now.

Hope your well as it leaves me at present.

Mrs Bostock."

" She hasn't punctuated it very well," Giles remarked, glancing over the letter which Miranda had put on the table.

" Don't you be so critical," Julian admonished, feeling he ought to. " If you don't look out, by the time you come to take your eleven plus, you'll know just what everyone else ought to do, and you'll miss getting a grammar school place yourself." He did not really think this. Two years before, Julian had got into a grammar school easily, while two years previous to that, Miranda had just managed it.

The girls minced up the end of the Sunday joint for dinner and to liven it up, Verna added a few herbs and flavourings.

" It's Shepherd's Pie ' a la Francaise,' " she said as Miranda served it out.

" What, frogs ? " Giles stopped with his fork uplifted.

" No, sorry, we were out of them so I could only put in things like red pepper and nutmeg and sage—— "

" I should stick to the jolly old Anglo-Saxon variety next time," Julian said, gingerly turning it over with his fork. However he and Giles both ate it up and each had another helping.

" Miss Hodges is coming at eight o'clock." Miranda skilfully cut up a large jam tart into four exact quarters. " We'd better offer her some coffee, Verna, and you'd better make it. Somehow I never seem to be able to make good coffee—it always tastes like warm sweet mud. That sounds like the gate."

It was a telegram addressed to " The Four Harveys " and read :

" Just going on board thanks for seasickness pills which I found in my pocket hope I shall have no use for them except to hand out in a superior manner to the other passengers but you never know forgot to tell you box of liquorice allsorts in sideboard drawer love Dad." Telegrams were his one extravagance.

There was a rush to the sideboard and Verna, who won by a neck, pounced on the box amid o-o-hs of satisfaction.

" We'll all have black tongues, like chows," said Julian blissfully chewing. " It's no use saving any—pass them round clock-wise, will you ? Anyone who likes those thin ones should be entitled to two at a go."

Miss Hodges turned up in a taxi that evening earlier than they had expected.

" The boys will carry up your things for you," Miranda told her, " and then perhaps you'd like some coffee."

" Well, I wouldn't say no to a cup ! I got off early to-day, and had a meal in town before picking up my cases."

As they all sat politely in the sitting-room while Miss Hodges and the girls had coffee, Miranda gave the new inmate a few particulars about life at Garrick Road.

" Dad left his spare key for you, and we leave one on that old bust of Shakespeare on the rockery—it fits nicely in his left ear—in case any of us loses one."

" If you get the knack of it, you can prise open the back kitchen window," Julian said, " but it means stepping into the sink, so Dad says no one over seven stone ought to." He looked her up and down, but was too polite to say what was in his mind.

"I never lose keys," Miss Hodges said firmly. "I think you can't be too careful."

"And then there's baths," Miranda went on. "The hot water system is a bit antiquated," she felt she ought to explain, "but you'll soon get used to the geyser."

"Sometimes the pipes give a gug-gug, or a kind of knocking noise," Giles informed her, "and if there's a burping sound in the hot tap it means that there's some air in the pipe trying to get out. You can't pat it on the back like you do to a baby, but if you turn the tap on a little it usually puts it right."

Miss Hodges was not impressed. "That's the worst of these old-fashioned houses—there are so many things to go wrong. Give me a nice contemporary bungalow. But then it takes all sorts to make a world and live and let live, I always say. Well now, I think I'll get my things unpacked, and I expect it is past this young man's bedtime," she said, turning to Giles. "My goodness, that hair's wasted on a boy! What some girls would give to have those dark chestnut waves!"

Giles went white with annoyance. He hated people remarking on his rather spectacular hair.

"I don't think it's so much wavy as that it won't stay down well, and I would rather you call it just plain conker colour, if you don't mind," he said with dignity. "And now as Mamie's back I'll get her bed ready," and he went upstairs.

"Who's Mamie? Another of you?" Miss Hodges looked bewildered.

"That's Giles's cat; she disappears now and then for days, but she always comes back. I think she disapproves of all of us except Giles—she'll do anything for him, but she just puts up with the rest of us."

"I don't know what Giles sees in her, because she's a scruffy-looking thing," said Verna. "And she's a bit anti-social. If you meet her on the stairs she'll probably walk right past you with that ' haven't been introduced ' look on her face."

"I always expect Mamie to ask me if I've brushed my teeth when she gives me one of her disapproving looks," declared Julian. "It's a good thing Giles gets on with her, or her feelings might be hurt at our lack of appreciation of her."

"I'm an animal lover myself, so I expect we shall soon get to know each other," Miss Hodges said, and proceeded to go upstairs to her room while the girls went into the kitchen to cut some sandwiches for supper. When they came back to the sitting-room, Julian was working on a model aeroplane.

"Ugh! Giles is giving Mamie that bit of treacle tart, with dabs of fish paste on top," Miranda said, shuddering. "And she's packing it away with evident enjoyment, and she's stopping every now and then to simply *drool* over Giles!"

"You know," Verna put in, "he goes round the stalls in the street market at Frinley, and spends some of his pocket money on fish paste for Mamie. It's bright pink and Giles thinks it's salmon, but as it's only fivepence a jar and just marked ' fish, ' I'm sure it's herring or something dyed pink. But Mamie loves it."

Just then the big tabby stalked in, looked round the

room and rather pointedly sat down by the bookcase with her back to them all.

"Look here," Julian said abruptly, "we shall be home all the holidays, and that week we had at Seahaven at Easter seems a long way off. Let's get up something each week—something a bit different, not just going off to the swimming baths, or cycling round."

"Sounds good—anything for a change from ' the daily round, the common task.' Got any ideas ? "

"Well, I did think that this week we might have a sort of tree-top supper party—— "

"Whatever's that ? " As Giles came in he caught the last words.

"We could have a hot supper after dark up in the three apple trees in the garden. We've all climbed them for years, so we know all the good niches and angles. If we invited Nicky and Jo Ann Weaver, that'ud make six— two to a tree. Of course, we really ought to cook the supper in the garden, but we'd probably get smoked out, and drop the sausages into the fire, and all that."

"We could have a fry-up and bring it all out at once in covered plates," Verna said enthusiastically.

"What about a few fairy lights in the trees ? We've got those off the Christmas tree, and I think Jo Ann could bring theirs."

"If we fixed a flat board on one of the boughs we could have the portable gramophone."

"A chap I know has a jungle record, with African music, and tom toms. He'll lend it to me, I'm sure. And we can finish up with a sing song—darky songs, and sea shanties."

Julian felt modestly pleased when he saw that the others

were keen on the idea. " Then what about Saturday ?
That would give us time to ask the others. Oh, and I
know what we can do ! "

" What ? "

" I'd better see if it'll work first." And as he sat eating
his sandwiches and drinking milk there was an intriguing
grin on his face.

An hour later, Julian crossed off the first day in red ink.

CHAPTER THREE

OPERATION " TREE TOPS "

THE NEXT morning Julian wrote the invitation on a piece of plane tree bark.

> " Please come to a Tree Tops Supper Party next Saturday. Seven Thirty. The Harveys."

The invitation was received with glee.

" Sounds fun ! " Jo Ann exclaimed. " If it's warm like this, it'll be lovely."

Nicky wrote an acceptance in tiny letters on a peeled willow wand decorated to look like a totem pole.

" Would some brandy snaps be acceptable ? " Mrs. Weaver inquired. There were whoops of joy, for her brandy snaps, treacly and crisp were delicious.

" I did think that it would be nice to have birds'-nest soup," Giles remarked, " as the supper party is being held in the trees—— "

" Why—have you tasted it ? "

" No. I just thought. I asked about it in Coulter's, but they said you can only get it at a Chinese grocer. Anyway, Verna said the very idea made her feel sick, so it might have been waste of money."

" You're telling me," murmured Nicky. " We'll cycle down the road with you, Giles. We're going to the village."

Giles was secretly flattered when Nicky and Jo Ann treated him as an equal since Nicky was fourteen and his sister thirteen.

They cycled up to the main road and then bowled along in the summer sunshine towards Penvale.

"We mustn't forget to call at Mrs. Bowyer's," Jo Ann called over to Nicky. "Mummy's making raspberry jam this afternoon, and she's run out of jam jars," she explained. "We're going to see if Mrs. Bowyer has any to spare."

"We can see masses of *luscious* raspberries over the wall at the end of our garden," Giles said. "But there's not a hope of us getting any, because we're not on speaking terms with Mr. Blake. Any ordinary neighbour would probably ask us over to have some."

"Is that quarrel still on?" inquired Nicky. "Does he still cut you dead when he meets you?"

"Yes. If he sees us coming along the road he crosses over. It makes us feel like lepers. I thought of taking a bell out one day, and when I saw him coming I was going to ring it and call out 'Unclean! unclean!' That would have made him feel silly! If he had crossed the road, it would look as if he really believed I had leprosy."

"And did you?" Nicky asked, grinning.

"No. Miranda said that it would be wrong to get a laugh out of lepers. So I only said as he passed, that in India, people of a low caste aren't allowed to walk in the shadow of people of a higher caste, and they have to cross the road. And he heard. Dad was very annoyed, and stopped my pocket money for a week. But it was worth it."

"Pity the feud doesn't die out," said Nicky.

"Umm. Honestly, we did try to be friends with him, but he won't believe it wasn't Julian who hurt his dog."

Mr. Blake was a writer who had come to live in Amberly

two years previously. Bay Tree Cottage, with its rambling garden, backed on to the end of the Harveys' garden. Simon Blake was a struggling writer, so he was glad to sell some of his fruit to the Penvale shops. Dozens of raspberry canes stretched up to the boundary wall.

Soon after he came to Amberly, there was the unfortunate affair involving his dog.

Mr. Blake was working in his garden when he saw a boy in a green blazer up among the raspberry canes. Laddie, the red setter, bounded after him. The boy, in a fright, threw a brick at the dog, then made off over the wall into the Harveys' garden.

Laddie did not recover from his injuries, and a furious Mr. Blake accused Julian, who hotly denied knowing anything about it.

Mr. Blake said angrily that although he could not prove it, he was sure it was Julian who was responsible. Simon was devoted to Laddie, and since that time, he had had nothing to do with the family over the wall.

" Miranda, let's draw up a list of food for the supper party." Julian strolled in at that moment. " Let's make fudge. Even if it is still warm when we eat it, warm fudge eaten out of a spoon sounds rather super."

" What about sausage rolls, and cheese straws, and Cornish pasties and—— " put in Giles.

" Cheese, that reminds me," said Verna. " I read the other day something you can do with cheese, ' fondue,' I think it's called, anyway, you cook it in a bowl, I believe, and it's all hot and runny, and everybody dips a piece of bread into it, and eats it like that."

" You'd better find the recipe, then. Mrs. Weaver has

promised some brandy snaps, so we'd better finish up with some jelly."

"What shall we have to drink?"

"We can have some bottles of milk, and straws, and orangeade for anyone who likes it, and Verna can make coffee if we want it."

"I say, will the housekeeping money stand all this, or will it mean lettuce and stewed apples for the rest of the week?" Julian remembered his responsibilities as man of the house.

"I was wondering about that," Miranda confessed. "Tell you what—if we each gave a shilling of our pocket money towards the cost that would help, and we could buy up any of the fudge that was left over, at sixpence a quarter."

"Sounds a bargain. 'Shop-soiled fudge, may contain a few squashed midges, or have been sat on, but otherwise in good condition.' We'd better have some fillers, like doughnuts, because the open air gives you an appetite. And anything over, we can have for breakfast, so it won't be extravagant really."

A sudden thought struck Miranda. "Look, do you think we should invite Miss Hodges? I don't suppose it would be in her line really, but she IS staying in the house."

The others looked rather blank.

"Perhaps we ought to," Verna said unenthusiastically. "Or her feelings might be hurt. But she wouldn't want to climb trees."

"She could sit at the foot of a tree and have her supper there." Giles usually had a solution. "In fact, if she's got a fur coat she could be one of the jungle animals we've escaped into the trees from. She might even have a tiger skin—that would be rather good, you know: 'Tiger, tiger, burning bright, In the forest of the night.' That's by William Blake."

"We all know that. You are not the only one in this family that's educated," Julian said automatically. "We'd better ask her, then. Giles, can you help me out in the garden? I want to fix up something."

Miss Hodges, when politely invited declined the invitation, saying that she preferred to have her meals on 'terra firma.' However, the next day she produced a tin of fancy biscuits and handed them over, remarking that when she was a girl they had tea parties in the afternoons, with games, but she supposed that times had changed, and that she hoped they would have a nice time.

On the Saturday morning the girls set to making sausage rolls and jelly. The boys were rigging up something in the garden, and when the cooking was under way the girls went out to see what was happening.

There were three apple trees at the far end of the garden. One stood near the corner, and the other two a few yards away at right angles, forming the shape of a capital L.

"Hey, what's going on?" Verna cried. Julian was up the middle tree fixing a stout wire to one of the branches while Giles, up another tree, was doing the same to the other end.

"I thought it might be fun to fix up an aerial railway for the supper," Julian explained. "Miranda, you'll want to be with Jo Ann, won't you? You two can be up here with the food—I've strapped up a shallow box to hold it all—Nicky and I will be up that one with the gramophone, and Verna, you'll have Giles with you, won't you? You could have the portable radio if you want it."

"Yes, but how is that wire going to work?"

"Well, instead of people having to come up and down the trees for more to eat, you can pass it along from tree to tree——"

"How do we do it?"

"Everything is passed along in a basket. See this?——" He hung a hook over the wire, then hung a wicker basket from the hook.

"Do we push it backwards and forwards?"

"We *could*. But it might stick half-way. I want something more professional. Throw up that ball of string, will you? . . . Thanks." He tied one end to the handle of the basket, then threw the ball across to Giles. "Pass it round a bough, will you? That's right—now throw the ball back to me." Giles missed, so Verna threw it up. Julian passed the string round his branch, cut the end and tied it to the basket handle.

"Now, pull one end of the string towards you, Giles— no, the other end . . . good!" The basket travelled steadily along towards Giles.

"Oh, jolly good!"

"We can dash out with the cheese ' fondue '—if I can make it—piping hot, nip up the trees, then pass the bowl round for everybody to dip their pieces of bread in, then pass it on again. Super!"

"What about drinks?"

"The bottles of milk can go round in the basket."

"And we can put coffee in Thermos flasks——"

"The sausage rolls would be nice hot. We'll put them

in the oven, and I'll slip in for them when we've finished the cheese."

They tried working the basket along in turns, and then the girls brought out old cushions which could be wedged into convenient angles to make comfortable seats.

" Golly ! it's twelve o'clock, and I'm supposed to be making a stew for lunch. Oh—the sausage rolls ! " They made a dash for the kitchen, wondering whether they would find rows of cinders, but fortunately they were just a golden brown.

Nicky and Jo Ann pushed their bicycles up the side way just after seven-thirty.

"Hallo everybody ! We remembered the brandy snaps," and Nicky put a generous sized box on the kitchen table.

" Do my eyes deceive me, or are we going to make fudge ? " Jo Ann recognised the ingredients spread about the kitchen, which had been tidied up for the occasion.

The fudge soon got under way, then, when it was done and had cooled down, everyone took a hand at beating the mixture until it was thick and creamy. Julian had greased two tins to pour it into, but Giles, who usually liked to help, had gone in search of Mamie without whom, he declared, the party would not be complete.

" Let's make half of it into coffee and walnut fudge," Miranda suggested. " There are a few shelled walnuts in the pantry—unless Giles has been at them—and a bottle of coffee essence. Get them, will you, Verna."

When half the mixture was safely deposited into its tin, Verna threw the walnuts into the remainder, then started to pour from the dark brown bottle. A screech from her sister nearly made her drop it into the basin.

" Verna ! Not that one ! That's *Worcester Sauce !* "
There was consternation in the kitchen for a moment.
Miranda gingerly scooped out a tablespoonful of fudge
with a blob of brown sauce on it, then gave a gasp of relief.
" I think it's all here," she exclaimed. " Thank goodness
no more was wasted. It was lucky I was not stirring."

Giles, who had come back into the kitchen after a
fruitless search for the cat, pricked up his ears. " Worcester sauce ? Mamie *adores* it ! Don't throw that
away, Julian ! " He went off with it on a saucer calling,
" Mamie, where are you ? There's some delicious fudge
with Worcester sauce for your supper."

" With all the queer mixtures that cat eats, I wonder
she doesn't come out in green spots or purple sploshes,"
said Julian. " But honestly, Miranda, I thought everybody knew by now that you shouldn't keep unlabelled
bottles about. They might have poison in them. We
don't want Dad to come back and find six corpses
stretched out on the kitchen floor."

" Seven, with Mamie," Giles murmured, for he was
back again.

The thought of all that fudge, *and* housekeeping
money, in danger of being wasted shook Miranda rather,
and she answered crossly. " Don't be silly ! We'd never
put poison, labelled or unlabelled, into the pantry !
Anyway, we don't keep any poison in the house."

" That doesn't matter. On principle, you shouldn't
leave unlabelled bottles about."

" Oh, don't fuss ! The label only came off the other
day—— Yes, you're right. I am a clot ! Giles, find a bit
of sticky paper and write it for me, would you please ?
And the coffee essence is on the second shelf, Verna."

When the fudge was safely out of the way Miranda turned her thoughts to the ' fondue.' " I haven't made it before," she said, " but we all like cheesy things, and as it was made in France a century or two ago in honour of some V.I.P. it ought to be all right. The recipe says that Monsieur Somebody or other recommended a bottle of the very best wine as an accompaniment to the ' fondue.' So if anybody feels like a bottle of the very best wine, there's no harm in asking, but I can tell you the answer beforehand."

She got busy with eggs, butter, cheese and seasoning and was soon vigorously mixing away, while her sister and Jo Ann sat on the table watching her. " I'm going to cook it in a double saucepan to keep it hot outside," she said. " Although whether the hot water underneath will survive its journey from tree to tree, I wouldn't know."

The boys went out to switch on the coloured lights which Julian had fixed among the trees. When the ' fondue ' was getting nice and runny, Miranda thought it should be nearly done, so she sent Verna on ahead to see that Julian had everything ready up in the trees, and to take out the doughnuts and fudge. " Put on something warmer, Verna," she said. " That woolly isn't warm enough. I don't want anyone to catch a summer chill." At the back of her mind was always the feeling that nothing must happen to harm the family while Dad was away—not if she could prevent it.

She cut some slices of bread into fingers, popped the sausage rolls into the oven to heat up, then called out, " I'm coming."

Jo Ann had gone on ahead and Verna had settled her up in the middle tree. As Miranda hurried down the garden trying not to spill the hot water in the double saucepan, the others cheered.

"Buck up!" Jo Ann cried. "I've got the basket ready, and I want to see how it works." Julian swarmed down his tree and handed the saucepan up to Miranda when she had ascended.

"You two have your dip first," he said, as he swarmed back on to the branch next to Nicky. "Then pass it on this way and we'll send it on to Verna."

Jo Ann had first dip and she pronounced the gooey mixture to be delicious. The ' fondue ' did the rounds, swaying along from tree to tree. Everyone, even the cook, approved of it.

"Why does everything taste so much nicer out of doors?" Nicky remarked, as he scraped out the last savoury morsel with the remaining finger of bread. "Can't you finish yours, Giles?"

"Yes, but I'm keeping this for Mamie. I'm sure she'll be along soon. I wish it was darker, then the coloured lights would show up more."

"Doesn't the grass look awful, with those bare patches?" Miranda said. "It reminds me of an old pair of shoes with the toes scuffed out. We ought to do something about it."

"It looks homely, anyway," Giles said shrewdly. "And scruffy old shoes are more comfortable than new ones. Julian—nip in for the sausage rolls, will you? And let's have a record on, Nicky. Let's try the jungle one, then if there are any moans, it will sound in keeping."

The gramophone was an aged one which squeaked when it was wound because they never remembered to oil it. The engine was liable to run out before the end of the record, so that a Covent Garden soprano might finish up a song in a series of moans and swoopings and changes of key which always sent Giles into paroxysms of mirth. Verna had a good ear for music and said this gave her the creeps, as it sounded as if the singer had suddenly gone mad, and she would violently wind away until the voice came back to normal.

" Don't put it on until I'm back," Julian called, and in a minute came back with a baking dish covered with a cloth. " Put the mustard in the basket, and mind the tin, Miranda, it's very hot."

The ' jungle sounds ' rang out, with distant strains of tom toms ; the wind instruments suggested the sound of animal calls ; cymbals clashed as if some elephant or rhinoceros were crashing through the undergrowth, and a jackal seemed to be screaming in answer to a hyena. It was perfect music for a jungle film background. It was dusk by now, and as the six of them sat there, they could almost feel they were on safari.

As Verna was dipping her last mouthful of sausage roll into the mustard there was a sudden spring from below, and a soft form jogged her arm and landed on the branch next to Giles. In her agitation Verna nearly fell off her cushion. She put the liberally coated morsel into her mouth for safety then choked over it.

" It's MAMIE ! " Giles cooed. " She's come just at the right moment—I knew she would. Look at her eyes shining like a panther's ! Here, Mamie you old pet, here's a bit of cheese dip for you." Mamie condescended to join the feast, and chewed up pieces of brandy snap with gusto, her tail thrashing out from side to side.

When the food was finished and the cold drinks were

used up they sat eating fudge and singing sea shanties. Miss Hodges' light was shining out from the top back bedroom window.

"Hope she doesn't think we're too rowdy," Miranda said, after a spirited rendering of 'Rio Grande.'

"She looked out and waved, a minute ago," Verna replied. "Perhaps she's even sorry to be out of it."

"There's no light in Mr. Blake's house," Giles remarked. "He usually works at the back—we can just see his light through the trees late at night. I'm rather glad, though. I wouldn't want him to come strolling up his garden to see what all the row was."

"He'd be a skeleton at the feast," Julian began. "Oh, I'd better not talk about him as I can never find anything nice to say about him."

"Oh—Mr. Blake!" Jo Ann exclaimed. "I wonder if it is the same one? Daddy was reading something in the evening paper a few days ago about a Mr. Blake whose car had been hit by a van and had overturned. This man was taken to hospital with concussion. It didn't give his address. Daddy read it out because he knew the spot where the accident occurred—where was it, Nick?"

"At Ribbleston Corner. The chap was taken to Ribbleston Hospital."

"I wonder if it *is* Mr. Blake? I haven't noticed him about lately. But I wouldn't know if he's away."

"The milkman would, if his milk was not taken in."

"He doesn't have anything left at the door—gets all his shopping as he wants it. I've seen him bring milk and bread and all sorts of things up the road."

They sang more songs, including "Old McDonald Had a Farm." The animal noises, which grew more hilarious with each verse, seemed to shock Mamie and she sprang down and disappeared into the gloom, a picture of offended dignity.

"Look at her," laughed Julian. "She's probably thinking, 'How silly can those humans get?'"

The sausage had made them thirsty, so they had coffee out of two Thermos flasks—even Giles, who did not particularly like it, but who did not want to be thought too young to enjoy it. "Let's finish up with the jungle record again," he said. "And let it make those moans at the end, Julian, it sounds marvellous. You can cover your ears if you're frightened, Verna."

"I'm not frightened!" she said indignantly, "I just hate it, that's all. But go ahead."

After the Weavers had gone and everything had been brought in from the garden, Miranda went down and climbed on to the marrow bed, from where she could see over the wall. It was dark and quiet, except for the chirrup of a sleepy bird. The heat of the day had brought out the scent of the raspberries in Mr. Blake's garden, a scent which always seemed to have something of rose petals in it, Miranda thought.

The Harveys' neighbours on the right were going away for their summer holiday in a few days; the house on the left had been empty for months. For the first time, Miranda was glad that Miss Hodges was staying in the house.

Suddenly, Dad seemed very far away.

CHAPTER FOUR

THEY DECIDE TO INVESTIGATE

" I WONDER if the Mr. Blake who was injured in the accident was our Mr. Blake." The Harveys were returning from church the next morning and had to pass Bay Tree Cottage. It had a deserted air about it, but as the owner was not what might be called a handy man about the house, the fact that the porch needed sweeping and polishing was no clue as to whether he was there or not.

" If it IS our Mr. Blake I hope he's not badly hurt, even though I don't like him," said Miranda. " Accidents always seem worse when you know the people."

"Perhaps Mrs. Tring at the Post Office will know," Verna suggested. " The village grape-vine seems to have its roots there. I'll ask her to-morrow."

They all had good appetites for Sunday dinner as, unfortunately, there had been nothing left over from the supper party, except fudge, so they had breakfasted on toast. They had sped their parting guests with a bag of fudge each, and what was left over they had bought up cheap, as arranged.

In the afternoon they were going to play tennis, but as it was so hot after dinner they sat about on the garden seat, and in two old, but stout deck chairs for a while.

" I say," Julian suddenly began. " I've been think-ing —— "

"Don't overdo it. You'll improve with practice."

" I've been thinking," Julian went on, ignoring the

ribaldry, " suppose it is our Mr. Blake, just about now he'd be picking all those raspberries and taking them over to sell to the shops in Penvale. You remember last year we saw him loading up punnets of raspberries into his old car one day."

" Yes, and Mrs. Tring says he takes them to Penvale because he can get a better price for them there—a lot of people round here grow them in their gardens, so there's not much sale for them in the village."

" Yes. Well—if he's got concussion badly he may be in hospital for a week or two. I mean, you hear of people being unconscious for days. And by the time he's out, those raspberries will be rotting on the bushes. Those that are ripe now, anyway."

" What's this leading up to ? " asked Miranda suspiciously. " You're not suggesting that we should go over and help ourselves, are you, rather than let them go to waste ? It might be some other Mr. Blake, and we'd look nice if we were caught at it."

" Don't be an ass ! Of course I didn't mean that," Julian said wrathfully. " What I was thinking was, that if it was him—he, I mean, we ought to do something about selling that fruit for him—— "

" *Selling* it ? " Verna sat up.

" Do you think we ought to interfere ? " Miranda said slowly.

" Mr. Blake's unfriendly, and he was beastly to you, Julian. It'ud serve him right if his fruit all went maggoty," Giles exclaimed, for that ripe fruit just over the wall was a sore point.

" Giles, that's uncharitable, when he may be unconscious and not able to defend himself ! " Verna said in rather a shocked voice. " It's like hitting a man when he's down." Giles looked rather ashamed and murmured, " Oh well, I hope they don't get maggoty, then."

" We could find out who the Mr. Blake is if we phoned Ribbleston Hospital," Julian went on. " They would probably give us his address if we said we thought it might be a neighbour of ours."

" How far away is Ribbleston ? "

" About twenty miles, I believe."

" How could we sell his raspberries for him ? Do you mean go over and visit him in hospital and ask if we may ? " Miranda sounded doubtful.

" No. It might give him a rise in temperature if he saw us walk in, complete with family feud ! We'd have to go over the wall and pick the fruit, and keep an account of how much we get for it."

" He might be *furious* when he found out ! "

" Well, I don't think that should stop us from trying to help him," Julian said doggedly. " We'll have to risk it. He may be a pain in the neck, but he's still a neighbour, and that's the sort of thing neighbours ought to do."

" I'm beginning to think it's a good idea." Miranda usually did think Julian's ideas good. " It'ud be easy enough to pick the raspberries, but how shall we know which shops he sells them to ? "

" And suppose the shopkeepers ask us where they came from ? They'd probably want to know, before they bought it. I know I would." Verna was surprisingly business-like sometimes.

" Humm . . . that's a point. We don't want the shopkeepers to think we'd pinched the fruit and were selling it on the quiet. Dad would go up in smoke ! "

"Look here," put in Giles, "let's find out if it's the right Mr. Blake first. If it isn't, all this planning is no good."

"It'll probably be a trunk call to Ribbleston. Let's scout round first and see if there's any sign of life at the cottage." Miranda got herself out of the garden seat. "I'll look over the wall, and you nip round the road and walk past the cottage, Verna. You're good at that sort of thing."

This produced no result, so Julian got through to the hospital. The others waited with the impatience which listening to a one-sided conversation usually produces. There followed phrases such as : "Yes . . . yes, thank you . . . no, I don't know which ward . . . Could you give me his address, please ? Yes . . . thank you . . . No, we're not relations . . . Yes, thanks, I'll hold on . . . I see . . . Thank you, Sister . . . good-bye."

"Yes, he's ours, all right. He's had bad concussion, but he's off the danger list. He's got to be kept very quiet, though, so he's to have no visitors unless they're relations. He'll be there another fortnight—oh, he's got bruised ribs, too. So I vote we get cracking about the fruit."

"I hope we shan't be had up for 'breaking and entering.' " Verna gave an uneasy laugh. "But I don't think it would be any more than trespassing if we didn't go into the house."

"Let's go over and have a look round."

They had forgotten about tennis. In a few moments Julian was sitting on top of the wall, then, with a spring, was over. "Come on," he cried. "I'll catch you, Giles. It's steeper this side."

"I can jump by myself ! " Giles answered indignantly.

" If you jump the professional way you don't hurt yourself." His 'professional' way landed him into some nettles which Julian had been at some pains to avoid, but Giles would rather put up with the stings than complain and invite ' I told you so ' from his brother.

Miranda and Verna over, the four found themselves creeping about and speaking in low voices. They could not help feeling that at any moment Mr. Blake might appear through the trees which grew between the house and the soft fruit up at the top end.

" I say, there are lots of canes ! " Verna exclaimed. " And look at the size of the raspberries ! If they're not picked soon, they'll be ruined."

" Let's get up early and begin before breakfast." Julian wanted to get the job started.

" No, they'll have the dew on them, and if you pick fruit while it's wet it goes mouldy."

Miranda had wandered off to the left. " Look, there are heaps of red currants here. Gorgeous for raspberry and red currant jam, or puddings ! But it's the selling that's bothering me. It's no good picking pounds of fruit if we don't know what to do with it."

" Shall we offer it round to all our friends ? " Verna suggested.

" No, Mr. Blake might not like it if he found out that we had touted his goods round the district."

They sat down under an apple tree, the fruit of which was beginning to turn a warm yellowy orange.

" I know ! " Verna exclaimed. " Don't let's take it to the shops. We can sell it along the roadside, like they do from the farms. You remember Dad bought some strawberries last year from a stall outside the farm by Great

Thrift. They had notices up about cut flowers, and honey, as well. If they can, why shouldn't we ? "

" That'ud cut out the middleman, certainly." Julian was remembering his arithmetic of the previous term.

" What does that mean ? " demanded Giles.

" Well, if a shopkeeper paid us ten shillings for raspberries, he'd sell them for, say, twelve and six. If we sold them to the customer, we'd get all the twelve and six, so we'd do without the middle man, between us and the customer."

" Julian, do you think we'd be allowed to sell along the road ? I believe hawkers have to have a licence, or something."

" Well, you are over fifteen, so you could be selling in Woolworths, if you wanted to, as far as the law's concerned."

" I'd better do the selling then, officially, but I don't suppose it would matter if you others took a turn. But whether you can stand by the side of the road and sell, just like that, I wouldn't know."

" Got it ! " Julian exclaimed. " Mrs. Bostock's sister Emm."

" *Emm* ? What about her ? "

" She lives out on the main road, doesn't she ? In that little flint cottage at the corner of Huntsman's Lane. Her husband is handyman up at the Hall. If they would let us have a trestle table by their front garden—— "

" How come a trestle table ? "

" Er . . . wooden boxes from the shed, with planks put across."

" I expect they'd let us keep it round the back instead of having to lug it home each time." Verna felt that they were getting organised. " I think it's a good idea about Emm's. Couldn't you cycle out there first thing in the morning, Julian, and ask her ? She might have some boxes and boards to lend us."

" I say ! " Miranda exclaimed, " We'll take the scales out, but what shall we put the raspberries in ? Bags aren't very good, because of the juice. They're always sold in baskets, or punnets."

" Oh gosh ! I don't believe you can buy those in the shops. I believe the gipsies make them."

" Bother ! We could try over on the common. But we'd need dozens of punnets—what do we use for money ? " Miranda was not going to part with the housekeeping money without a struggle.

" Dear, dear, what a fuss ! Leave it to your Uncle Giles and follow me." Giles sauntered towards the house. Near the side wall was a potting shed and he peered through the window. " While you were nattering I was looking round a bit more. See those ? "

On the bench were piles of baskets and punnets, and a pile of tissue paper. " He was all ready for the season, I should think."

" Good show ! And even if it does mean ' breaking and entering '—— " The door was locked, but after fiddling about with a penknife, Julian managed to loosen the window. " There, we've burnt our boats, so in we go."

They scrambled in and, although they were now on enemy ground, Miranda realised that they had got their normal voices back.

" What do these baskets hold, Miranda ? Two pounds ? "

" Yes. And the punnets a pound, I should think—— "

Verna gave a sudden screech, " There ! Look there——! "

For a wild moment the three others expected to see Mr. Blake peering through the window towards which she was pointing, but when she gasped : " That spider ! That huge one ! " they were reassured. With Verna it was spiders ; with Miranda, mice, and oddly enough it really seemed to give Julian the creeps if he heard moths flapping about in a dark room. Giles had a secret fear of bats, as he had heard that they entangled themselves in your hair, but as Dad wouldn't let him have a crew cut he had to hope for the best, and remember to mention it in his night prayers when he thought of it.

Julian neatly caught the spider's thread on one finger and deposited it gently out of the window. When order was restored, Miranda said, " Do you think we had better weigh the fruit here, or take it over in baskets, on our bicycles ? "

" That's going to be awkward. It's a mile and a half, and we'd have the raspberries bouncing out into the road, if we weren't careful . . . If only one of us had a driving licence . . . "

Julian caught sight of some gardening tools, and that gave him an idea. " Listen—there's a chap down the road who cycles along to the allotments—I've seen him on Saturdays. He takes his tools in a kind of little trailer fixed to the back of his bike. I wonder if he would hire it to us ? We could take that out of the profits as expenses. I don't suppose it would cost much, and we could get it back to him by the time he would want it in the evenings."

" I think that's a brainwave ! It'ud be worth paying out a bit for the transport. Oh, has anyone noticed the price of raspberries in the shops ? " No one had, so it was decided that each one would take on a job. Julian was to call on the man that evening. Miranda would cycle out to Emm's in the morning; Verna would go down to the village shop and find out the price of the fruit, while Giles was to wash the kitchen scales and take them over to the shed.

That evening Julian returned very jubilantly. "He says we can borrow the trailer, and he won't make any charge. In fact, he says that rather than unfix it each time, I can borrow the bike. I didn't tell him it was not our fruit, but he seemed to know who we were. He says if we get the bike back by six each evening that would do."

"Good show! Did you see it?"

"Yes. It's got small rubber wheels, and it'ud take about ten baskets, I should think."

"What I want to know," Giles said earnestly, "is whether it is honest to eat some, if it's not our fruit."

"Seeing that it's a physical impossibility with most people to pick fruit and not eat any, it's always understood that you can. But if you get tummy-ache in the night don't wake me," Julian said.

"Cold meat and salad to-morrow," Miranda said briskly. "And the other jam tart. Giles, while I'm gone you run the vacuum over, will you? And Verna, there'll be four sheets and a tablecloth to go to the launderette, won't there, but they'll have to wait until Tuesday."

Just as Miranda was leaving after an early breakfast she shouted back: "What's Emm's other name? I can't call her that."

"I've never heard anything but Emm."

"Isn't it Claydon? Oh no—that's Win, her other sister."

" Oh, just call her Mrs. Er . . . er," Giles suggested.

" It's POSGATE. Thanks. 'Bye."

In an hour things were moving.

" She was jolly co-operative," Miranda announced. " She found two boxes, and an old door to go across, because they hadn't any planks. She says we can use their shed. Verna, did you find out the prices ? "

" Yes—two pound baskets of raspberries are four and six, and the red currants were one and ten a pound."

" Gosh, what a price ! We'll make his fortune."

" Come on, I'm dying to start," cried Giles. " I've put out basins for everybody."

In a moment they were over the wall.

CHAPTER FIVE

OPERATION "GOOD NEIGHBOURS"

THE RASPBERRIES hung in clusters of great tempting berries, warm from the sun. The four picked steadily, only stopping now and then to pop a particularly juicy specimen between lips already stained a deep carmine.

"Some of the best ones are underneath the leaves," Verna called over to the others. "If you get low down you can see lots that you might miss."

"He's looked after them awfully well," Julian remarked. "I've seen hardly any grubs, and only one or two of those little red spiders that you usually find on raspberry canes."

"*Grubs?*" Miranda hastily examined the berry she was just going to put in her mouth. "Ugh! I didn't think of grubs! I haven't examined any of the raspberries I've eaten."

"Well, what's a grub, more or less?" Giles said nonchalantly. "They are probably quite nourishing. Anyway, it's the grub you should be sorry for—not yourself. One minute it's sitting nice and snug on a great soft juicy red cushion and the next moment it's being put into a great cavern. But I expect death is instan . . . instantaneous. It probably dies of fright when it sees the size of your mouth."

"My mouth isn't big!" Miranda said indignantly. "Your mouth may be smaller, but you talk twice as much. Any grub coming near your mouth would probably think

53

it was a loud-speaker with a sports commentary coming
out of it full blast."

" How are we doing ? I vote we weigh what we've
picked." They weighed two pounds of fruit, then tipped
it into a basket lined with tissue paper. Then Miranda
thought of a better way. " We don't want to keep transferring them from one thing to another—they'll get
bruised. Let's pick into the baskets and weigh them in
it."

" There won't be two pounds of fruit, then."

" We'll weigh a basket, then add that weight of raspberries."

" It'ud be easier to put a two pound weight AND a
basket on one side of the scales, and a filled basket on the
other. The two baskets would cancel each other out."

" That's some kind of algebra, isn't it, Julian ? " Giles
asked. " A plus B equals something or other," he added
hopefully.

Julian sighed. It was no good trying to put Giles off,
but really, algebra in the summer holidays ! " Yes, when
weight plus basket equals fruit plus basket, fruit must
equal weight.

$$W \text{ plus } B = F \text{ plus } B$$

" Why isn't it all A's and B's ? What's W ? "

" The two pound weight, fathead ! "

" Oh yes, I see."

Julian went over the wall to write a notice for the stall,
and to bring back bread and honey for elevenses, while
the girls discussed transport. Verna suggested taking the
fruit down Mr. Blake's sideway, and loading the trailer in
front of Bay Tree Cottage.

" No fear ! " Miranda was emphatic. Suppose Constable Merrick should be passing, can you imagine trying to explain away twenty five pounds of fruit, in marketable baskets ? No, we'll have to get it over into our garden."

There was a call from Julian. "Come and get the doorsteps, will you ? They'll probably fall honey-side-down into the nettles if I jump."

As they sat contentedly munching Julian said, grinning wryly, "Sorry I was so long—I had to do the notice again. I spelt ' raspberries ' without the ' p ' ! I felt like a wretched little first-former."

" Good thing you noticed. We may be suspect thieves over this fruit—we don't want to be thought illiterate as well."

They got the baskets and punnets over the wall and into the trailer, with a plastic tablecloth, won in a raffle but not used because it was so hideous, strapped over to keep out the dust.

"All ready ? Who's got the notice ? Let's get going, then."

To the tune of ' Strawberry Fair,' the most appropriate tune they could think of, the convoy set out. Julian had to negotiate the bends carefully, and he was never sure what would happen if he should slow down, but they did quite well.

" We're coming to the hump, then that sharp dip over the bridge, Julian," Miranda called. " I should get off—you might find the trailer turn into a bucking bronco." Julian thought caution was certainly called for rather than endanger twenty five pounds of fruit so he got off and pushed until they came to level ground.

By the time the four reached the Posgates' cottage it was nearly midday and very hot. They soon had Emm's old door across two tea chests which had been filled with firewood for the winter. Emm had obligingly let them stack the wood in a corner of the shed. They set out the baskets, propped up the notice and awaited customers.

A car sped by, filled with a family obviously returning from the sea. A cry went up of " raspberries ! " and back came a gentleman who carried off a basket.

" We must have an account book," Miranda said as she put the money into a spare punnet.

" I've got a note book I've hardly used. I'll find it when we get home," Julian promised. " Look here, we must push the red currants. They won't sell so easily." Next a cyclist dismounted, took one look at the price, grunted and rode off.

" We must come out earlier to-morrow," Miranda declared. " We don't want to be here until three, and then have to go home and get ourselves a meal. And we don't want to come back this afternoon. We'll have to lower the price if they don't sell."

" Bad business," said Julian. " We must improve our salesmanship. I'll try a bit of patter on the next passer-by."

" All right. Here comes the oldest inhabitant. Exercise all your charm—you'll need to."

" Can I interest you in these, sir ? " he began, per-suasively holding out a sample in each hand. " Guaranteed all fresh, and a lovely flavour. Beautiful for jam, and—— "

" I've been growin' fruit before you was born," said the ancient. " Forty year, man an' boy," he added, peering disapprovingly at the counter. " No call fer me to buy any. Forty year, man an' boy. All I wants I grows." And with a snort he shuffled past. Julian looked slightly flattened. "Evidently the wrong approach. But this one looks more likely."

A smartly dressed lady was coming along. Julian repeated the patter but she gave an apologetic smile, shrugged her shoulders, flung out her hands in an expressive gesture and produced a stream of what might have been Arabic. Julian was left speechless.

"Your charm must be slipping," Miranda said sweetly. "But perhaps these children will fall for it." However the children sidled up to Miranda and asked for "three pennyworth, please, Miss." She regretfully had to refuse the sale, as it would have left one basket short weight.

By half past one they had sold seven baskets and two punnets, and they were all feeling hungry.

"Verna, you and Giles had better go home," her sister said. "Get some tomatoes to have with the cold meat, will you? And pull a lettuce. Oh, and I can't face fruit for lunch. We'll bring in an ice cream block, and it WON'T be raspberry flavour."

Left to themselves, Miranda and Julian resolved to push the sales. The next passer-by seemed hypnotised by Julian's flow of sales talk and went off in a daze with one basket and one punnet.

"So the old charm hasn't deserted me," Julian said, grinning. "Here comes another car." This time their luck was in. Two ladies bought the remaining fruit for jam, and then the two behind the counter thankfully carried the table top and the tea chests round to the shed. They called out their thanks to Emm through the kitchen window, then triumphantly set off for home.

After lunch they sat under the apple trees to discuss Operation 'Fruit Pickers.'

" Here's the account book," Julian announced. " We're doing fine and dandy for a start. Ten two pound baskets of raspberries at four and six : two pounds five. Five pounds of red currants at one and ten a pound : nine and two. Total, two pounds fourteen and twopence. Nothing on the debit side yet. But we may run out of baskets, and then we'd have to get some somehow."

" If we find we're getting short we can offer threepence on the basket if it's returned."

"Yes. Now, what about to-morrow, Miranda ? There was a fair amount of ripe fruit still on the bushes."

" Well, we needn't all go over. If you'll cope with the trailer you could go straight back. I'll sell, but I'd rather like someone for company."

It was decided that they should all go over to Emm's, then Giles would stay with Miranda, and after Julian had unhitched the trailer he and Verna were to go on to the swimming baths. They would leave about one o'clock, and come back to the stall to see if there was anything to pick up.

There was nothing to pick up except the trailer. The others had gone home, and announced gleefully at lunch time—shepherd's pie and pancakes—that for some reason sales had been much speedier.

" Eight baskets at four and six," said Giles, " that's one pound sixteen. And four pounds of red currants, that's seven and two—— "

" ——man and boy, I've been doing sums for eight years, and I've always said four times one and ten is seven and four. I've always said that, man an' boy, for eight years. I don't hold with these new-fangled ways of counting—— "

"All *right*, then. Seven and four. Enter it in the book, Julian, and tell us the total."

"Humm . . . Takings to date: Four pounds seventeen and sixpence."

"I say! That's properly money for jam!"

Verna, who had gone to answer the phone, came rushing back. "Listen, do you think we could give to-morrow a miss? It was Sally Hunt, Miranda, she wants to know if we—you and I—can go with them for a picnic. Wardle Valley, and then on the river."

Julian said that as they had picked the ripest fruit, it would be a good thing to leave the picking for a day or two. He would take Giles to the county museum, if he liked, so they could all have a day out. Verna dashed back to accept, and when she finally appeared after a long chat with Sally, Miranda had had an idea.

"You know the Hunts, Verna! They'll take a big picnic lunch, and then have us back for a whacking great tea afterwards. And they won't let us pay for boats, or anything. We could take some raspberries as our contribution, and pay out of the housekeeping money. It'll be good for our sales, too."

"Good idea. Two pound basket? If we asked for the basket back we need only pay four and threepence."

"Yes. We'll pick them in the morning, but I'll pay for them now before I forget. *Where's* that housekeeping purse?"

"It was in the knife box when I dried up," Giles declared. "You probably had your reasons for putting it there though I can't think why."

"Oh, nobody would look there," Miranda said vaguely. "Not even myself when I lose it!" She threw over four and threepence to Julian who entered it into the book and put it with the rest of the Blake money under a pile of magazines in his bedroom.

The girls decided that some housework must be done if they were to be out all the next day. Verna flew round upstairs and gave the bedrooms a rather superficial " do," while Miranda washed over the kitchen and polished the hall. " U—gh ! " she thought as she straightened up her aching back, " this is the way to keep down those inches round your hips—and to get housemaid's knee."

When Verna came down the girls did the washing except for the heavy things. When the family wash was out on the line Miranda said that she would take the sheets and towels to the launderette. " And I'm too tired to wander round the shops for half an hour while the things are boiling," she declared. " I'm going to stay there and sit with the Mums and knit. It's time I finished that jumper I started last winter."

The next morning, while Miranda was picking raspberries, Verna cut sandwiches for the boys, who were planning to see a travel film after going to the museum.

The day passed off pleasantly but uneventfully since everything went according to plan. They all got back about the same time, and sat round listening to a radio programme while Julian and Giles had baked beans on toast—dull, but necessary, Miranda said, since they had not had a proper meal out. They heard Miss Hodges come in and plod upstairs, then, not long after, they could hear sundry thumps coming from her room.

" Wonder what she does ? " Julian remarked idly. " I've heard that noise before."

"She does cook sometimes, I know. I'd say she was banging a steak to make it tender."

"A *snake*?"

"No—a *steak*, idiot. All the best chefs do it."

"I'd say she was practising country dances. You know—'Hey nonny nonny, tra la la, thump, thump.'"

"I believe she has a printing press up there, for forging money. She'll be uttering forged pound notes any time now, though why you utter them I don't know. I should think you'd keep quiet about it. I should. What do you think, Giles?" Giles's theory was that she was building a small-sized rocket from a "do it yourself" kit, and would become the most famous woman scientist since Madame Curie, and that was why she had jumped at the offer of a room at the top of the house. She would fire the rocket out of her window, and it would bring back sensational information from outer space. When she was dead—which would be before many years, Giles added, as she was fairly old now—there would be a plaque put on the outside of the Harvey house: '"Ethel Hodges, famous scientist, once lived here.' And—— "

"——Yes, end of chapter one," Miranda put in, although quite kindly. "It's time you rocketed off to bed, Giles. I promised Dad. And I say, we must be careful what we say about Miss Hodges, even when we are just making things up for fun. If she heard us talking about her like that, she might think we were awful. And you should never hurt the feelings of people staying under your roof."

As they were locking up for the night Verna, looking out of the kitchen window towards the deserted garden of Bay Tree Cottage, said that if they did as well on Friday, their next intended fruit picking day, they could feel jolly pleased with themselves.

"Don't be too complacent," Julian said. "Anything could happen : fire, tempest, earthquake—— "

"Not an eclipse," put in Giles. "I've looked it up. The next one is ages ahead."

The next day Julian was to remember his own casual remarks.

CHAPTER SIX

TRAGEDY—AND A CRISIS

THURSDAY STARTED off as a lazy day of pottering. The boys got up early because they liked getting up. Miranda came down at eight o'clock, while Verna strolled into the kitchen about nine, made herself toast and took it into the garden with some orangeade.

"Let's enjoy ourselves to-day," Miranda said later. "No—*not* on the draining-board, Verna. *Wash* them, we've done our crocks long ago."

They swam in the morning, then sat reading under the trees after lunch.

"I'm going to tidy up the borders," Miranda announced suddenly. "There's some rubbish we can burn." They cut down straggling forsythia, piled weeds on dead wood, and soon had a good heap.

"It'ud blaze well if we put paraffin on," Giles said hopefully.

"No fear! Too dangerous. It'll burn up with newspapers."

A moment later a match was put to it, and immediately flames sprang up.

"Hey, be careful!" Julian warned, as Giles prodded it with a rake, making it spread towards the fence dividing their garden from their right-hand neighbour's.

"There's some old matting in the shed," Verna called. "I'm sure it encourages rats."

" You've got rats on the brain, Verna," jeered Julian.

" They'll be good company for your bats in the belfry,"
his sister answered calmly. She dragged out the dry
matting, and flung it on the flames.

" It's catching the grass alight—stamp out the sparks,
Giles ! " The acrid smoke made their eyes smart, and it
was difficult to get near. Soon flames began to creep
hungrily up the fence.

" Get a bucket of water ! " Julian shouted. " I'll go
and fix the hose on."

The boys dashed over to the garage. The hose, rarely
used, was very stiff. With difficulty they unrolled it and
Julian turned on the tap. Meanwhile Miranda had
thrown one bucket of water over the flames, and drenched
Verna's arms. " Ow ! " she yelled, and shot round, only
to get a gush of water full face from the hose. The girls
directed the jet on to the flames, and they began to die
down. Five minutes later there was a blackened, sodden
mass, and burnt out fencing for a distance of about ten
feet.

" We are prize idiots," Julian remarked. " It was too
near the fence."

" It's my fault really," Miranda said bitterly. " I lit
it."

" We were *all* in it," Verna said with a groan. " What
a thing to happen when Dad's away ! Whose fence is it ? "

" The Northwoods'. They had it renewed about three
years ago."

" That makes it worse. If it were our side, Dad would
say what complete asses we were, and would patch it up
with a few odd planks and it would have to do until the
whole fence was nearly ready to drop down. As it is, he'll

have to pay for the damage. I'll *hate* having to tell him about it. He'll feel that he can never leave us on our own without something happening . . ."

"Let's find out how much it will cost to replace," said Julian. "Do you remember who put it up? If so, I could find out the price."

"It was the men from Eastons' wood yard," Giles told them. "I made friends with the foreman. He showed me how electric saws work, and he gave me a lot of sawdust."

"I'll go and measure up." Julian finished drying his arms and went in search of his father's steel rule. "Who had it last? Nobody ever puts it back—Giles, you were using it to measure your bicycle wheel."

"No, you had it on the landing when you were mending the cupboard door."

"Here it is, in its proper place." Miranda pulled it out of the dresser drawer from under some dusters. "If only you'd *look* properly before arguing . . ."

They went over to the scene of the disaster and Julian had a look. "There are sections, with a post every five feet," he said. "These two sections will have to be renewed, although the last foot of this one isn't damaged. Let's see . . . it's six feet high and the uprights are longer but I don't know how deep down they go. Anyway, they'll probably know down at the wood yard if I describe it. I won't say where it's for, in case they ask awkward questions. I'll cycle down straight away."

Half an hour later he returned looking rather gloomy. "I asked the foreman in the office about the price of fencing, and he said they had an illustrated leaflet which gave all particulars, so I didn't need to mention addresses.

This seems to be the kind. Here—' Interwoven fencing, in four widths, with posts.' "

"That looks the sort," Miranda agreed. "Let's go and compare it."

There was no doubt that 'Type IIB, six feet high, by five feet wide' was the fencing the Northwoods had had put up.

"Gosh! forty five and six each section!" Verna groaned. "And it needs two sections."

"AND a post," Giles added glumly. "How much are they?"

"Nine and six. That's . . . let's see—twice forty five and six is four pounds eleven, and nine and six . . . five pounds and sixpence. We'd better offer to put it up ourselves, to save the cost of labour."

"Look—don't let's leave Dad to face the music when he comes back," Miranda said suddenly. "In any case, the Northwoods are coming back on Saturday, so we'd have to tell them then. Let's deal with it ourselves. Let's use the emergency five pound note—it IS an emergency— and slip it into the Northwoods' letter box with a letter, for them to find when they come back. And we can tell Dad he can deduct it out of our pocket money over the next few months."

"Yes. He'd probably let us down lightly, but it would be a gesture on our part. If we've any pocket money left by the time Dad comes back, we can perhaps put a pound back. But my money seems to dribble away, what with swimming, and that." With the best intentions, they could not raise all the money within the next three weeks, Julian felt.

"Julian, get down the Saint Christopher picture, will

you ? " When he had peeled back the sellotape and taken away the new, crisp note, there was a depressing blank. " Well, that's that," he exclaimed. " Still, if I came back and found that neighbours had burnt my fence, I'd feel better about it if the money to pay for it was in the letter box. Come on—let's write the letter."

Between them they evolved the following rather formal letter. The Northwoods were quite nice elderly people, but rather ones to ' keep to themselves,' and the Harveys did not see much of them.

' Dear Mr. and Mrs. Northwood,

We are so sorry that we inadvertently burnt down some of your fencing to-day when we had a bonfire. From the enclosed leaflet which we got from the Wood Yard we find that two panels of IIB fencing will be needed, and one upright, costing five pounds and sixpence altogether.

We enclose the money with our apologies, and will be glad to fix the fencing for you when you get it.
Yours sincerely,'

" We'll all sign it," Miranda said, putting her name to it. " Where's that five pounds ? And three halfpence from each of you, please, and I'll change it into a sixpence."

Verna went round with the envelope and when it fell with a little thud into the letter box, she wondered if there was any way in which they could make some money for themselves. They were busy making it for Mr. Blake !

When she got back the others had dragged the garden seat across the gap in the fence. Miranda said that they did not want Miss Hodges to start asking questions. "No, she might get up on her hind legs and think she ought to let Dad know there has been a fire," Verna agreed.

"Oh well—it's no good worrying over it," Miranda went on. "But if anyone can think of a way for us to augment our income, let the rest of us know. I didn't dare borrow from the housekeeping money—Dad said that was to be used for housekeeping ONLY."

The next morning there was a minor earthquake in the post. Giles always went down if he heard the postman, and he came up with two letters, one from Dad, and the other in Dad's Aunt Eleanor's handwriting. They read Dad's first.

He was dazed with the hospitality and seemed to spend his time bowing from the waist; he had made the Americans an offer for the Empire State Building but they had regretfully declined his offer, saying that they had got used to having it around; he already knew a dozen new slang American expressions, but that it was like learning a foreign language; if they caught him chewing gum when he got back they could fine him sixpence. He felt sure they were being reasonably sensible over meals and bedtime, and he hoped they were having a bit of fun. He said that the Americans always seemed to be rushing about in a great hurry, but that they lost time over words like braces, which they called suspenders, and lifts, which were elevators with them. He also said that the American kids were cute but not a patch on his. They all had a nice kind of feeling when they had read it.

Miranda opened Aunt Eleaner's letter rather in trepidation. She wondered whether it would be full of instructions and advice on how they should manage while Dad was away, but that was not the reason for her letter.

She said that she was going to a concert at the Albert Hall that evening, Friday, and would be staying with friends for the night. She thought she would take the chance to pay them a visit on the way, and see how they were getting along in their father's absence—he had sent her a post card from the boat. She would be coming by car, and hoped to be with them about twelve o'clock. If they had any previous engagements they were not to alter their plans, however, and if they were not in she would go straight on to Town.

As Miranda read aloud, her thoughts ran on ahead. She saw a busy day in front of them, but not the sort they had planned to have. One thing was certain : they would have to give the day over to Aunt Eleanor, for after all, she had been good to Dad when he was a boy.

The letter produced consternation and some argument.

" What about picking the raspberries ? "

" We'll have to leave them for to-day. We can't all just disappear and leave her ringing on the doorstep."

" But she said if we had another engagement—— "

" People say that, but they only mean things like dental appointments, or being invited out for the day." Miranda did not look forward to the visit but she felt she must uphold the laws of hospitality. " She's quite nice really. It's just that we don't see much of her, so she seems more like a visitor."

" If only she wasn't so keen on everything being spick and span," Verna complained. " You know how she used to say that you could eat off her kitchen floor. That was until she heard Giles say, ' Who would want to, anyway ? ' "

" That was years ago, when I was six," Giles said, going pink. " You couldn't expect a boy of six to have a complete set of manners. I wouldn't say that now—at least not so that she could hear it."

" She is a bit fussy," Miranda admitted. " House-proud, they call it. We'll have to set to and practically spring-clean the place in the next four hours. She likes to be shown all round. There's one thing, she can't go into Miss Hodges' room. Oh, *lunch !* "

Miranda was getting flustered. She had a suspicion that Aunt Eleanor felt that Dad should marry again. If she found the place what she would call uncared for, or meals out of tins, she would probably talk to Dad about his duty to his four motherless children. She began biting her left thumb-nail, a sure sign of agitation, which Julian noted.

" A plan of action," he said, " is what is needed. Grab me paper and pencil, Giles, and Miranda can give out jobs. Four people working four hours each : that's equivalent to one person working sixteen hours. It works out more, as a matter of fact, when it comes to bed-making and such jobs. Mrs. Bostock would spit 'n polish the whole house, *and* cook a meal, in less time than that."

The girls brightened up.

" Thank goodness we washed on Tuesday, Verna, so the boys have clean shirts. We'd better wear our ginghams."

" I'll have to wash mine, then, it's got a stain down the front. It'll dry in half an hour."

" We'll have sole, and peas, and chips, and . . . oh,

and a raspberry and red currant pie. Giles, would you pick a pound of each ? That'll be . . . four and a penny. Here it is. We'd better do it properly and get some cream. Is there any coffee ? "

While Verna was at the wash tub Julian began a vigorous clean through, declaring that he would sweep, mop and polish, but that he drew the line at dusting which he thought was a waste of time anyhow. By eleven— and there was not time for elevenses—the house reeked of carbolic, floor polish and brasso. Mamie, routed out from her favourite corner on the kitchen cabinet, walked disdainfully past Julian, put one paw into the tin of floor polish, licked it and went out to the bottom of the garden.

" Will she look into cupboards and drawers ? " inquired Giles, his arms full of such things as old catalogues and empty tins for which there was no specified place.

" No, she wouldn't do that. But don't bury things too deeply or we'll be looking for them for weeks."

Verna let her dress get too dry, damped it down and then forgot about it when she got back from the village with the shopping. As she dumped the things down on the kitchen table she noticed how dingy the windows were. " If only that wretched window-cleaner had been round ! " she grumbled. " Mrs. Bostock said he was due. I'd better give them a wipe inside—that'll help."

Tempers were getting rather frayed. Miranda shot the fruit into the pie dish, having given only a mere glance for spiders and grubs. " Oh—get out of my way, Giles, will you ? Get some marigolds for the table and the hall, and give the porch a mop over, I want to do the veg. before Aunt Eleanor arrives."

Ten minutes to zero hour Miranda was laying the table,

and rearranging the flowers which Giles had jammed into a vase. "We'd better change now," she called out. Verna, who was wearing old tartan trews with a ripped hem, gave a groan as she remembered her dress, and reached for the iron. The boys were ready with their hands fairly clean, and when the door bell rang Verna had just got into her dress. "You go, Miranda," she cried. "This dress is still *steaming!*"

When they sat down to lunch Miranda felt justifiably proud. She was not really so very keen on cooking, except when she felt like it, but this time everything had turned out perfect. Aunt Eleanor seemed agreeably surprised at the meal, and enjoyed Verna's coffee. The "tour of inspection" afterwards also went off well, as the aunt did not ask awkward questions, nor peer too deeply into anything. "You seem to be tackling the housework quite well in the absence of your help," she remarked. "The place looks nice and fresh and polished." Miranda thought guiltily of the dead bluebottle she had kicked under the hall chest as she had gone to let Aunt Eleanor in . . .

Tea was only a cup of tea and biscuits as Aunt Eleanor firmly refused anything else, since she was dining with her friend before going to the concert. She seemed quite gratified when Julian showed an intelligent interest in music and was able to discuss the "New World" Symphony with her.

"I must see if we can arrange for you and Miranda to come up to the Albert Hall to one of the 'Proms', if your father is agreeable. The two younger ones can have their turn when they are a little older."

Just before she left, Aunt Eleanor thanked them for

giving her such a pleasant time, and she gave Miranda a pound note to share among them.

"It's funny how people seem nicer if you have taken some trouble over them," Verna said thoughtfully, when they were having a real tea. "Not funny ha-ha, but funny strange. The last thing I wanted to do this morning was to chase round like a mad thing, but it was worth it."

"Yes. I hope she tells Dad we showed up well. He'll be like a dog with two tails."

They were just finishing tea when there was a knock at the back door. It was the window-cleaner . . .

CHAPTER SEVEN

THE HARVESTERS ARE ANXIOUS

THE NEXT day there was a letter from Mrs. Bostock. Miranda had routed out a few magazines and had posted them to her, knowing how she liked them. Miranda read the letter to the others over the scrambled eggs at breakfast.

" Dear Miss,

Thank you ever so dear for the magazines which I always say its nice to have a book handy if you have nothing else to do. They arrived just before we left Lindford for as you see I am now at Sandstone Bay as my sister and her Bert had arranged to go there for a week, and the landlady had a spare room.

It is quite nice here altho the advert said a stones throw from the sea. If the stone could dodge round the tower of the Civic Centre and then go over a block of flats it would get to the sea eventually, but thats as it may be.

I'm having a nice time dear and my leg is healing nicely. We went on the pier yesterday and Bert won a pair of vases at the Aunt Sally, just nice for their mantelpiece. Then we went to the Show in the pier Concert Hall, the Dinkie Doodlers, dear, talk about a scream.

I think the sea has gone to my sister Win's head for she has bought herself a pair of trousers slacks she calls them bright pink dear, and not really for anyone who wont see thirty again. What I say is you have got to have the figure.

Don't forget to turn the mattresses once a week dear Friday I always did them. And if your looking for the caster sugar its in the big jar marked tapioca seeing has you never have tapioca and it holds two pounds of sugar nicely. I keep mixed spice in the jar marked caster sugar. If your in any difficulty over the house write to me dear and if I can help will be glad to oblige.

Must go now dear as we have high tea at six. All very nice really but theres nothing like your own food I always say.

Mrs. Bostock."

" Isn't she an old dear ? We'll have to remember those mattresses, Verna—we can't let her down when she's taken the trouble to mention them. Now, let's go over the wall directly we've done the necessary chores."

"After yesterday's upheaval we can leave the house to settle down and recover for a few hours," Julian remarked, skilfully transferring a spoonful of honey, with a golden stream already beginning its slow descent, on to a slice of toast.

They had got up later than usual and had pottered over breakfast, so it was nearly ten when they found themselves among the raspberry canes again. As they picked industriously, Verna found herself looking nervously behind her from time to time. " Do you think we could phone Ribbleston Hospital to see how Mr. Blake is ? " she said suddenly. " I'd hate to see him walk up the path from the house."

" I'd been thinking that," Julian said. " Miranda, you could phone while I'm getting the trailer. We'd know then how long we could safely come here."

The last two days had been very hot with a few hours' rain one night, and that had produced berries of a wonderful size, and full of juice. The baskets were filled in a shorter time, and before they realised it they had picked twenty two pounds of raspberries and eight pounds of red currants.

" How gorgeous these currants smell ! " Giles said, with an ecstatic sniff. " We should do well to-day, because people will be doing their shopping for the week-end." Just then Miranda came back from the house and reported that Mr. Blake was getting on well, but that he would not be coming out of hospital for another week. " We shall probably get all the fruit picked by then—except a few late canes. It's all ripening more or less at once."

When Julian called over that the trailer was ready, Miranda told the other two that they needn't all go to Emm's, because she and Julian could cope, and why didn't they go for a cycle ride ?

The four went off together, and as they drew near the main road there seemed to be a subtle change in the weather. It was still and close ; Miranda had a headache and wondered if this meant a storm on the way. " I wish we had listened in to the weather report," she called over to the others. " I don't like the look of it over there. Let's try to get rid of all this as soon as possible, even if we lower the prices. It's half past eleven already."

" Yes," Julian called back, " I promised Mr. Merrick that I'd bring back the bike by one o'clock on Saturdays as he goes to his allotment directly after lunch."

As they set up the counter storm clouds were gathering, and there was that ominous flutter of leaves in the trees, and the low flying of birds which showed that the rain would not hold off for long.

Cars whizzed by ; walkers hurried along anxious to get under cover, and no one seemed interested in the stall.

"Let's cut the prices," Julian said suddenly. "We don't want all this fruit on our hands. We can write on the back of the notice—I've got a black chalk pencil somewhere . . . Shall we say two shillings a pound for the raspberries, and we'll sell a pound if they want it? There's a pair of scales in the shed. And one and six for the currants?"

They propped the boldly chalked notice prominently, and soon a car drew up and a basket and a punnet changed hands.

"Here's the rain!" Miranda exclaimed as the car drove on. "Let's put the plastic cloth over the baskets. I wish we hadn't picked so much! It was lovely at breakfast time though. Nobody thought of rain." They stood under the porch, slightly sheltered from the weather. Emm and her husband had gone down to Sandstone bay for the week-end, so there was no one to ask them in, although the shed was open. The wording on the notice was starting to run and passers-by could not tell what was for sale under the cloth.

It was really coming down by now, and as a water-proof enveloped cyclist came into view Miranda in desperation ran out to the path and called out : "Raspberries, fresh picked this morning, two shillings a pound." The gentleman bought a basket, probably out of the kindness of his heart, the two thought, and strapped it on to his carrier.

Miranda found some newspaper in the shed to cover it with.

The rain, which the farmers were welcoming with delight, fell steadily. Suddenly there was a low rumble, then a flash of lightning. Miranda and Julian were getting soaked, so they hurriedly carried the baskets into the shed. They had sold four baskets and two punnets.

" It's half past twelve," Julian said anxiously. " I *must* get the trailer back by one o'clock, come thunder, lightning and tempest. Mr. Merrick will hardly go up to his allotment to-day but I promised."

" Look here, we'll have to take it all back," his sister said. " I think it'ud be a waste of time if I stayed on my own—it might rain all day, and how could I get the remaining fruit back ? It'll have to go on the trailer, and we had better start now."

Feeling rather disgruntled, the two of them set off. The rain was lashing down, and the thunder and lightning more frequent. Julian dumped the baskets down by the Harvey front gate, then cycled on down the road, leaving Miranda to take them inside. When he got back he found Giles and Verna wheeling their bicycles up the side way, and when the three got into the kitchen Miranda ordered everyone to change into dry things.

" We got as far as Stornton Cross," Giles began, " and then it came down in bucketfuls."

" Go—— ! " Miranda ordered. " I don't want everybody down with pneumonia. And don't start shouting down to know which shirt to put on."

" All right. If I can't find one I'll put on my pyjama jacket."

" ——and change your *socks !* "

"All right. If I can't find any I'll borrow Verna's purple bed-socks."

"I haven't *got* any bed-socks!" Verna shouted back indignantly. "I wouldn't *wear* the beastly things! And as for purple—— "

"Pipe down," said Julian. "You ought to know Giles by now."

Verna had gone down to the village before she started fruit-picking that morning, so in half an hour they were having hot sausages. While they were finishing up with gingerbread and cups of tea Miranda broached the subject which was in all their minds.

"Twenty pounds of fruit there," she said, waving towards the pantry. "And what are we going to do with it?"

"Can't we sell it on Monday?" Giles asked doubtfully.

"It'll be going mouldy by then—it's fully ripe now, and very juicy; even by the morning there'll be some mould on the top . . . I don't like the idea of setting up a stall on a Sunday morning. And I'm sure Dad wouldn't approve, either."

"After all, we are not responsible," Julian said slowly. "We weren't to know the weather would change. It's still pouring, by the way."

"We could buy some ourselves," Verna suggested, but rather half-heartedly. A treat which is almost compulsory loses its charm . . . "It comes rather expensive, though, and raspberries always seem to need cream— that puts it rather in the luxury class. Besides, twenty pounds . . . Would it be dishonest to give some away?"

Julian looked rather bothered. "It's one thing to help a neighbour, but we've added trespassing, and 'breaking and entering,' even if it is only a shed. And to give away other people's goods . . . it might be counted a form of stealing, by law."

Giles, who had had his dreamy look on his face for some minutes turned round and said, simply : " Jam."

The others looked at him blankly. " Jam ? "

" Yes. Couldn't we make it into jam ? "

Miranda looked alarmed. " But I don't want to spend two pounds twelve out of the housekeeping money on fruit—and that's without the sugar—Mrs. Bostock makes us damson, and plum, and that's much cheaper—— "

" ——and sell it on the stall," Giles went on calmly. " People always buy jam at the Church Bazaar. I bet they'd buy ours, if we labelled it ' Home Made Raspberry and Red-Currant Jam.' "

" Giles, that's an idea ! " Verna looked at her young brother with respect.

" What about it, Miranda ? " Julian inquired. " It's not everyone's idea of a summer holiday."

" I think we could." Miranda looked relieved. " At any rate, we'd be on the right side of the law. The thought of any trouble with the police while Dad is away curls me up. Imagine him returning to a family of Juvenile Delinquents ! "

Julian jumped down from his perch on the kitchen table. " We'll all be in this. Do you know how to make jam, Miranda ? "

" Not really. But there are some old cookery books in the dresser drawer somewhere. I wish I hadn't dropped cookery to take extra Science . . . " She rummaged about a moment. " Here, Verna, you take one and we'll compare recipes."

Verna spread herself out on the floor. " Gosh ! " she exclaimed, " We'll need twenty pounds of sugar. That will cost over twelve shillings, won't it ? Can you lend it out of the housekeeping money ? "

" Oh dear—yes, I suppose so."

" Don't be daft," cried Julian. " It can come out of the cash in hand from the fruit we've sold. Will we need anything besides sugar ? "

" It says here ' mash up the raspberries with a silver fork '—— "

" What, *real* silver ? We haven't got one. And why should it have to be silver, anyway ? "

" Perhaps it's something to do with the acid."

" I'm not buying any silver fork—not even with the cash in hand. We'll use a fish fork then—they're the ones in the best condition. This book says : ' Add half an ounce of butter to each five pounds of fruit.' "

" Whatever for ? "

" ——' to prevent the scum rising.' Ugh ! sounds horrid."

" This book says : ' Heat fruit, then add the warmed sugar. When dissolved, boil until set '—whether that takes five minutes, or an hour, I wouldn't know."

" Mine says : ' Add sugar to fruit, let it stand two hours, then boil three minutes.' "

" We can't wait all that time ! It's muddling, reading different instructions. I vote we take the best of each recipe. Giles, could you see if there are any jars in the cellar, or in the shed ? "

" Verna, you and I had better go for the sugar—we can carry ten pounds each on our bikes. I'll go upstairs for the money." While Julian ran upstairs Verna found some ancient shopping bags to hang over their handle-bars, and Miranda started to stalk the red-currants. " Golly ! " she suddenly cried, " There'll be forty pounds to boil up, counting the sugar ! We'll have to have several boilings."

Giles managed to find twenty-seven jam jars in different places.

" It's lucky Mrs. Bostock used to keep some," Miranda said, looking up from her stalking. " Who can we ask for some ? Put on your mac, will you, Giles, and cycle down to the Hansons. Oh, and Miss Pratt, you know, down Elmhurst Lane, might have some."

By half past three Miranda had washed out the big pan which Mrs. Bostock used occasionally for making jam for the Harveys. On the window-sills stood a row of freshly washed jam jars, forty of them, and on the table, twenty pounds of sugar, a little butter and a fish fork. Miranda looked at the array and had visions of burnt jam ; running jam; jam that had lost its colour, and jam stiff as cheese. All that fruit . . . and all that sugar . . .

" I think I'm beginning to lose my nerve," she said.

" Never say die ! " exclaimed Julian. " Up, the Harveys ! What do you do first ? "

" We'd better do it in four batches, then. I'll weigh out five pounds of fruit, and Verna, put five pounds of sugar to warm. It had better go into the oven, to speed it up."

Miranda shot the fruit into the pan, giving it only a perfunctory looking-over, and mashed away vigorously, refusing to think of anything that could crawl or fly that might be there . . . It looked and smelt wonderful, especially when the warmed sugar was added.

" Giles, read out that bit about the sugar, will you ? "

" ' You must not bring the pan to the boil until the sugar is dissolved.' "

" Hi, shouldn't those red currants have been stewed ? " Julian had just noticed them on the dresser.

" Heavens, yes ! Stick them in a saucepan with a little water, will you ? Now we'll have to wait ten minutes. Oh well, the sugar can be dissolving. I'll put about a pound of the currants with each boiling."

" Then you'll have to take some raspberries out, or you'll bring it up to six pounds, and we've only warmed five pounds of sugar."

" Bother ! " Miranda took down a jug, baled out some of the mash and put the same amount of currants in the pan. " There ! "

" Half a mo." Verna grabbed the butter and dug a lump off then slipped it into the pan where it melted immediately. She had found a wooden spoon in the dresser drawer, and gave it a stir.

" ' Boil briskly,' " Giles quoted, " so you'd better turn the gas up."

The fruit was soon bubbling nicely. They left it for a moment to compare recipes, until Julian sang out a warning : " ' Way, ay, and up she rises,' " and dashed over to turn the gas down before the jam boiled over.

They tried a few drops on a saucer to see if it would ' jell,' and at the second try, after seven minutes, got a lovely crinkly fold. " It's done ! " they cried in chorus.

" We haven't heated the jars," Giles added calmly.

" Drat ! We'd better heat some water and pour it into each. That won't take long."

They each took a turn to bale out the jam with an old cup and pour it into the dried jars. It really looked marvellous.

" Delectable ! " said Julian, sniffing. " I always thought that that bright red jam in the shops, with each pip showing, was too good to be true and that they put cochineal and chips of wood in, to make it look the real thing. But look at this ! "

" Greaseproof paper to cover the pots with ! " Verna remembered with urgency. " We must get it before the shops close." They sent Giles hurriedly down to the village then started off on the second batch. This was not all plain sailing ; the pan had cooled, leaving a gluey coating all over the surface. They scoured it off in case it should burn. When the next five pounds of fruit seemed to be done they began to feel that there was nothing to it, until Julian said, doubtfully, " It's filled ten pots, and the last lot only filled nine."

"Perhaps I didn't boil it enough," Miranda said frowning. " I don't think it jelled quite as much. Drat ! Better give it another few minutes."

They had forgotten all about having tea. When Giles came back they were just filling jars from the re-boiled jam. Mamie sidled in between Giles's legs, got under Verna's feet and caused her to jog her sister, who was filling a jar. A stream of hot jam slid and nearly made her drop the cup. Some hot juice spurted on to her hand and when the jar was safely on the table she stood ruefully examining a red burn.

" *Why* are we doing this ? " she suddenly said in exasperation. " We don't even *like* him ! " But they couldn't not do it. No, they all felt that.

Now that they were half-way through the job, they decided to go on and finish, rather than start again after tea. The third boiling took longer to set, probably, they thought, because there was less red-currant in it. The last five pounds gave no trouble and by six o'clock the four of them stood, hot and dishevelled, around the table on which there were thirty-four jars neatly tied down and labelled.

"We seem to have been an awful time," Verna said. "It isn't the cooking so much, is it? It's the getting ready, and the fiddly jobs."

"AND the trial and error," added Julian. "I've put the scrapings out from the pan into that basin, Miranda, but I feel I don't want to look another raspberry in the face for a long time. It'ud give me the pip."

A chorus of jeers went up from the others. "One out of ten for that pun," Verna cried, "and that 'ud be generous."

"Yes, it is pretty awful," Julian admitted. "It's funny how, even if you hate puns really, you can't seem to help making them yourself sometimes."

Just as they had decided to have a 'high tea' of sardines on toast and to open the packet of chocolate biscuits, bought for Aunt Eleanor's visit and not needed, there was a knock at the kitchen door. It was Miss Hodges, ostensibly to ask if it would be convenient for her to take a bath then, without upsetting any of their arrangements. She gave an appreciative sniff.

"You've been busy, I see," she said, looking over Verna's shoulder. "Raspberry jam, by the smell, and what a number of jars! I suppose it's none of my business——" Miranda looked alarmed. When people said that, it usually meant that they were going to make it their business. " ——but did I see you climbing back over the wall at the bottom of the garden this morning, with some baskets of fruit ? Have you some arrangement with the neighbour ? "

" Well . . . not exactly," Miranda said. There was nothing else she *could* say.

" You didn't take all that fruit without permission though, did you ? " It was Miss Hodges' turn to look alarmed.

Julian felt that half explanations and evasions were no good, and that for the sake of the family name they would have to tell her what had been going on. He offered her a chair and started, and each of the others put in bits as it occurred to them. " . . . and so we are going to try to sell the jam at the stall next week," Miranda concluded.

" But do you think your father would approve ? " Miss Hodges asked. She looked rather dazed from the conversational bombardment to which she had been subjected. " I did not take on any responsibility for your behaviour while I am here, but you seem to have undertaken a great deal. If this poor man is in hospital, perhaps the police could have dealt with it . . . they could have got the W.V.S. to have done something about it, I should think," she said vaguely.

" Oh Miss Hodges, don't bring the police into it, please ! And who are the W.V.S. anyway ? " asked Giles.

" Women's Voluntary Service," his sisters said together.

" Well, we are the Harvey Voluntary Service," Giles went on, " and so long as the work gets done, that's all that matters." Miss Hodges could not stand out against

Giles, whose dark eyes were full of tragedy. "Well, I suppose you've got so far, you might as well finish the job," she said doubtfully.

"We are only trying to help a neighbour," Verna said virtuously, forgetting for the moment that up to then, Mr. Blake's name had been mud in their estimation.

"We are keeping proper accounts," Julian said. "When the fruit is sold we are giving the money over to Mr. Blake. It's run on a non-profit basis, as far as we are concerned."

"I'm sure you meant well. I'll buy two pots from you," Miss Hodges said unexpectedly.

"Oh THANK you, Miss Hodges! We haven't thought about the price yet."

"I'm afraid I can't help you about that—I'm not very domesticated. But you should charge more for it than the bought jam. Let me know when you decide on the price." She went off with her two jars and the Harveys started on the toast for the sardines. "That was decent of her," Julian commented. "I thought we could quieten her down, but I didn't expect to make a sale. Only thirty two more pots to sell."

"Only!"

"What I want to know," demanded Giles earnestly, "is what became of the other six pounds?"

"What other six pounds?" Verna wondered if they had overlooked any fruit. Surely there was not another batch to do!

"There were twenty pounds of sugar and twenty pounds of fruit. Why didn't it make forty pounds of jam?"

"It boils down and a lot of the water evaporates."

" Gosh ! six pounds of water rising up and floating out of the window ! I should think—— "

" Stop thinking and come and get your toast.   Three sardines for each person." Giles, murmuring : " Triplets on toast, Sardeena, Marleena, and Dargeena," scooped his three out of the tin. Soon the comparative silence showed how hungry they were.

" I've got to enter this up," Julian said, at the chocolate biscuit stage.   " What are the expenses ? "

" Sugar, eleven and eight . . . the butter doesn't count. I suppose we could charge up the gas."

" What's gas sold in ? Therms ? " Verna asked vaguely. " Oh yes, cubic feet. We don't know how much it took."

" Let's say sixpence. Then the greaseproof paper : sixpence. We're throwing in the three dozen jam jars free."

Julian got his accounts satisfactorily made up, except for pricing Miss Hodges' two jars. That night, as he crossed off another day on the calendar he said, " Dad's been gone nearly a fortnight. We must write to him again to-morrow. Don't let's mention anything about over the wall—it's too involved. It'll do when he gets back. Where's Giles ? I want to lock the back door."

" He's out in the road, searching for Mamie. He says all this shooing her out of the way has been bad for her nerves. He took the sardine tin with him, to lure her back—he says the olive oil will give her vitamins and make her coat shine. I nearly suggested he got her a bottle of Parrish's Chemical Food but I didn't want to hurt his feelings."

CHAPTER EIGHT

"HAPPY BIRTHDAY TO YOU!"

THE NEXT morning the Harveys found great satisfaction in the sight of rows of jars on the kitchen table.

" It looks gorgeous! " Verna sighed. " I couldn't eat a scrap yesterday—we seemed to be floating in a sea of red juice—but let's have the scrapings on our cornflakes."

Coming out of church at midday, they saw the Weavers. Nicky and Jo Ann had returned the previous night. Giles sought out Mrs. Weaver and went straight to the point.

" How much is home-made raspberry and red-currant jam, please? "

Mrs. Weaver, who was very musical, was still thinking of the organ voluntary which seemed to have transported her to heaven, but she tried to come down to earth.

" Jam? " she repeated vaguely. " Do you want to buy some, poor lamb? I can *give* you a jar—— "

" No," Giles explained patiently. " We've got thirty-two pounds to sell."

" To *sell*? " Mrs. Weaver looked startled, so Verna joined in to explain.

" Well, I'd charge one and tenpence a pot. I made lots this year, or I'd buy some."

Giles finished his job by politely waylaying Miss Hodges when they got back and collecting her three and eightpence.

After Sunday dinner, which included slightly burnt

89

custard which Julian said made him feel he was back at school, Miranda reminded them that they were all helping at the church Garden Fête the following Saturday week. "There's to be a 'pets' competition," she added. "A shilling entrance fee, and two prizes—one for the pet with the most appeal, the other for the one with the most personality."

"*Any* pets, like performing fleas?" Giles asked hopefully.

"You're not keeping *fleas*, are you, Giles?"

"No, I just thought it would be fun if somebody brought some." Giles walked away thoughtfully. The others could see what he was thinking: "Mamie!" they said in unison.

"Wonder which class he'll enter her for—appeal, or personality?" Julian remarked with a grin.

"She's got personality, all right," declared Verna. "She looks like a disapproving school teacher usually. We mustn't make too much fun of Mamie, though, or it'll hurt Giles's feelings."

"No. He'd burst with pride if she won a prize!"

"Now," said Miranda, "we must take the jam out to-morrow. Let's go early. I'm afraid someone may ask if we have a licence, or something."

"Don't frown so! Your forehead looks like a piece of corrugated card!" Julian teased.

Miranda laughed. "Well, you know what I mean! There's the phone. It's your turn, Verna."

The usual tantalising bits of conversation floated in, then Verna suddenly shrieked: "*Six* o'clock? Six in the morning?" There was some giggling, then Verna came in grinning broadly.

" It's Jo Ann. We're invited to a breakfast party—— "

" Breakfast ? "

" Yes. Six in the morning. Agonising ! I don't think I'll go to bed the night before. She says will Wednesday do ? Right, I'll tell her. It won't be at their house—it'll be on the invitation where."

When she finally hung up, Verna found to her satisfaction that the washing-up was just finished. A great calm descended as they settled down to write to Dad. Miranda's was lengthy and rather cautious, because she did not want him to start worrying ; Julian's, brief, and rather dull, for all his ideas deserted him when he was staring at the notepaper. Verna's was loving and a bit muddled, while Giles wrote four pages describing in great detail the airliner he wanted to design to put all others in the shade.

In the morning, Miranda and Julian went off to Emm's with the jam, and some fruit. The other two were sent off to the baths, but were told to be back by one o'clock.

They had forgotten that it was bank holiday Monday. Most walkers were making for the picnic spots, and carried quantities of packed lunches. Cars sped past on their way to the coast, and everyone seemed to have stocked up well in the food line.

By midday they had sold five baskets of raspberries, and three jars of jam.

" Twenty nine jars left," Miranda said thoughtfully. " Of course, what we don't sell, we can put in Mr. Blake's shed and let him know how they came to be there. But I'd love to make a good job of it and for us to get rid of the lot. Let's see—when is he coming out of hospital ? "

" It could be about next Saturday, by what they said."

" I wouldn't mind buying one jar for ourselves, out of the housekeeping money, but I'm jolly well not going to buy all that's left over, even to oblige him. Oh, here's one of our girls coming along. Gosh, it's that wretched little second former, Mavis Jones—she's in my House, and she's always had a bit of a crush on me. I hope she won't hang about too long."

The girl on the bicycle caught sight of Miranda, turned bright pink, wobbled a bit and got off.

" Oh, hallo Miranda," she said, looking with adoring eyes. " Are you having nice holidays ? Do you live round here ? I thought you lived near Amberly."

" Yes, so I do. But we're helping out someone who is ill—selling his garden produce for him. Oh, this is my brother Julian." Mavis went a brighter pink still and could only produce, " Oh, are you ? " The thought of speaking to Miranda's brother left her tongue-tied. " I could help you, if you like," she said, squirming with sudden shyness.

" It's all right, thanks. We'll manage."

Mavis dashed home to ask her mother to buy some fruit, and was soon back clutching four and sixpence for a basket. " I think I'll buy a jar of jam too," she said. " I'll give it to Granny for her birthday."

" Oh, Mavis, you needn't ! It was sporting of you to buy the raspberries."

To be told that she was ' sporting ' by a prefect, who was also Miranda, almost overcame Mavis who turned nearly the colour of the fruit. " But I'd love to buy it ! It's my pocket-money." Miranda could do nothing but hand over a jar, and Mavis went off glowing.

" Well, you've made her day," Julian said with a laugh.

" She's helped to make MINE! That leaves twenty-eight jars. What's the time ? "

" Nearly twelve. Let's stay until half past, then put the rest of the jars in the shed."

Emm and her husband were still away, but the shed was never locked so they carried the remaining jars inside and put old newspapers over them, in case of prowlers.

Over the remains of the Sunday joint, helped out with a salad made by Verna who had spent half an hour decorating it, and which disappeared in a flash, Giles announced : " It's Miss Hodges' birthday."

" How do you know ? "

" There were two cards for her on Saturday. One had roses on, and ' Happy Birthday ', with ' for Monday ' inked in. The other had violets and a sundial, and : ' Happy birthday to my Cousin, May your joys come by the dozen. Begone all sorrow and repining, May Life show its silver lining.' "

" Gosh ! What a shocker ! You seem to have had a jolly good look."

" I didn't read the private part the other side, Julian ! " Giles said indignantly. " Anyone's allowed to read the front."

Just then Miss Hodges came past the window and asked if she might hang a cardigan out to dry.

" Why, of course."

" Happy Birthday ! " added Giles. " I hope you had some nice presents."

Miss Hodges looked embarrassed. " Oh, I never get presents now," she answered with a little laugh which somehow didn't sound the right kind. " I get cards from two elderly cousins—my only relatives. Well, I must be getting on," she added vaguely.

"What a dull birthday!" Verna remarked. "I should *die* if my birthday was no different from any other day. Couldn't we give her something?"

"The shops are shut . . . I've got a handkerchief box that Jean gave me. I'll get it." When it was found, the words: A PRESENT FROM NEWQUAY stared up at them across the lid.

"We can't give her that," Verna declared. "It looks like someone else's cast off. What about that scarf I had given me last Christmas? The colour didn't suit me and you didn't like it, but Miss Hodges might."

Miranda and Julian contributed ninepence each, so as to share in the present and Verna found that, oddly enough, although she had provided the present, she ended up with a profit of one and sixpence.

"I'll give her something on my own," Giles said. "I'm going to make her a birthday cake."

"*Make* her one? But you can't!"

"How do you know I can't? I can follow instructions from a book, the same as anyone else, I suppose?"

"But you'll spoil it. You'll waste the ingredients——"

"Why should I? I helped make the jam. And anyway, it was I who found out that it was her birthday."

Miranda realised that this last fact had rather gone to Giles's head, but she did not want to spoil his satisfaction.

"All right, then, you can try. But you'd better do it on your own because personally I've had enough cooking lately to last me for the rest of the hols. There are some cookery books in the dresser drawer."

Giles lay on his stomach on a balding patch of grass and

studied the books at some length. At last, when he seemed
to be torn between Dundee cake, and "Festive Cake,"
(five eggs, and half a wineglass of rum) Miranda felt she
should come to the rescue. "We haven't got some of
those ingredients, Giles," she told him. "Why don't you
make a sponge sandwich? You can put it together with
jam, and there's just enough icing sugar in the pantry to
do the top."

Giles studied the recipe and finally decided on it. As
he went towards the kitchen Julian said, "When he makes
up his mind to do something he just goes on and does it
and practically nothing will stop him. We'd better leave
him to it."

Just then Nicky and his sister came up the side way
with their invitation. Jo Ann held out a folded paper
which, when unfolded, had KEEP OFF THE GRASS
written on one side. On the reverse it said:

"Please join us at the entrance gate to the Jubilee
Gardens at 6 A.M. on Wednesday 5th. Sports and
Competitions. 7 A.M. Hot breakfast. 8 A.M. Cycle ride
to Chippenham Valley returning to US for elevenses."

This produced animated conversation.

"But where will we have the Sports? The Gardens
are all flowerbeds, and you have to keep off the grass, as
you know."

"That's why we thought it would be more fun—to do
something unexpected," Nicky explained. "Old Ted
Farrow, the caretaker, opens the Gardens at six o'clock in
the summer, because a few people use it as a short cut to
the station. And Harriers use it sometimes for practice

runs. Ted is a great one for ' rules and regulations '—you have to be out of the place the moment it's closing time, and all that. Well, there's no regulation saying you can't have egg and spoon races along the paths, or a treasure hunt."

" I shall feel I've done a day's work by the time we get back here after elevenses," Verna commented. " I shall feel like going back to bed."

" Nothing to stop you, sluggard."

" Yes there is, we've got to go out to Emm's, and then again on Friday for a final clear up. We've got twenty-eight jars of jam to sell." Nicky did not offer to help pick fruit, as he felt that the Harveys did not like taking other people on to the Blake territory, but he did suggest that they should have elevenses at half past ten, so that there would be time to pick the raspberries and take them over after early lunch.

When the Weavers had finally torn themselves away and gone off to play tennis with friends, Miranda went in to see how Giles was getting on. He was standing by the table, the tip of his tongue out and an ecstatic look on his face, turning out one sponge round out of the tin.

" That looks marvellous, Giles ! " Miranda exclaimed, looking at the pale golden circle on the rack.

" I just went by the instructions," Giles said rather smugly. " It only needs common sense. I'm waiting for the other round to finish cooking. Mamie, move over a bit. You shall have something special for supper later on."

But Mamie was in one of her restless moods and a moment later, as Giles was carrying the second sponge round over to the table, Mamie darted across the kitchen after a fly. Giles tried to avoid her and stumbled;

Miranda endeavoured to catch the cake, but the tin shot out of Giles's hands and landed on the floor upside down. He quickly picked up the tin, but the sponge was in pieces.

" Oh—that wretched Mamie ! " Miranda cried in exasperation before she could stop herself. " She will get under people's feet ! "

Even in the moment of disaster Giles remained loyal.

" It's not her fault ! She wasn't to know it was important. Oh—go away, Miranda, don't stand there ! *Go Away !* " he shouted, stamping in frustrated rage.

Miranda wanted to help, but she knew that Giles was near to tears and simply hated anyone seeing him cry. She went back to the others who were still lounging in the shade and reported what had happened. " Wasn't it maddening for him ? And they both looked beautiful, just right. Odd, isn't it ? Even when I take pains my cooking is never anything special—except when Aunt Eleanor came, and the patron saint of cooks must have been looking after me that day—but Giles makes a cake with no help, and gets perfect results. Beginner's luck, I suppose."

Ten minutes later Giles came out. His face bore traces of the recent tragedy, but there was quiet triumph in his manner.

" Couldn't we ask Miss Hodges to have tea with us, Miranda ? She can't have her birthday cake all to herself. Then you can give her your present."

" I should think so. We can have it out here. Did you ice the one layer ? I'm sure she will be pleased with it."

" The cake is all right," he said with a knowing look.

" I'll go and ask her to come—I've heard her upstairs."
He came back saying that Miss Hodges would be pleased
to come. " I thought perhaps she didn't want to at first,"
he said, " because she had such a queer look when I told
her we had a surprise for her. You said quarter to five,
didn't you ? Don't come into the kitchen for ten minutes
anyone, please."

The girls came in later to put the kettle on and to take
out the tea things, while Julian in a burst of energy cut
bread and butter. The cake, Giles said, was in the pantry
and not to be seen.

When tea was ready Giles, dancing with impatience,
went up to escort the honoured guest down. She was
rather " on ceremony " at first and Miranda felt as she had
done the first time Miss Hodges had come to tea, when
each side felt the other to be on trial.

" Give her your present and then I'll bring mine out,"
Giles cried, and that broke the ice. Miss Hodges was
obviously surprised to receive a present and fumbled over
the parcel, but when she saw the scarf she seemed
delighted.

" It will be just right to wear with my new two piece,"
she said with great satisfaction. " The colour will tone
in beautifully. Thank you so much."

" Now I'll get mine," Giles said importantly. He ran
off and came out a moment later bursting with pride.

" It's a birthday cake. I made it for you," and he held
out what was obviously a two-layer cake, with white icing
and rather sprawling words across in bright pink.

Miss Hodges again had that " queer " look on her face
which Giles had seen earlier, and she could not seem to
get any words out. " For . . . for me ? I . . . I . . .

Excuse me, I hope I'm not getting a summer cold," and she blew her nose.

"It's a Mosaic Cake," Giles announced. "I made up part of the recipe myself. You put jam on the bottom piece, then you break the top round into pieces . . . or anyway, it's broken up, and you put the pieces on top of the bottom layer, fitting them together again like a jigsaw puzzle. Then you colour each piece a different colour. I used red and yellow jam, and cocoa powder, and honey, and a little bit of lemon curd I found. This makes it look like mosaic, you see? And then I iced it."

They all leant over to see, and sure enough, through the white icing various colours could be seen faintly. The pink wording said :

HAPPY BIRTHDAY
FROM
THE HARVEY'S

"It's . . . it's beautiful!" declared Miss Hodges. "I've never had a birthday cake before. Thank you very much, it was most kind of you!"

Giles hustled up the serving of tea and the passing of bread and butter, anxious to reach his masterpiece. When it was time to cut it, Miss Hodges looked quite pale with the solemnity of the occasion. Rather to everyone's surprise it tasted very nice. They all had second helpings, and left a small piece for Miss Hodges to have the next day.

When tea was over a slight touch of formality returned.

"Thank you for a very pleasant time," Miss Hodges said. "And thank you once again for the scarf. I shall always remember my birthday tea," she told Giles. " It was kind of you to take all that trouble. Thank you."

" I believe she's LONELY ! " Julian remarked, when she had disappeared into the house. "Perhaps that's why she seemed bossy at first. Perhaps bossy people feel they've to throw their weight about, to get themselves noticed," he said shrewdly. " She doesn't seem to have many friends."

" No, she doesn't. I'm glad we did something for her to-day."

They started to take the tea things in. Giles went on ahead with a pile of plates.

"A Mosaic cake ! " Verna said, grinning. "Trust Giles to turn a fiasco into a new invention ! There's one thing about him—he won't accept defeat."

" Did you notice the wording on the cake ? " Miranda murmured so that Giles should not hear. " FROM THE HARVEY'S, with an apostrophe S ! I remember how I was always getting that wretched apostrophe wrong when I was his age. ' When in doubt, put one in, to be on the safe side,' was my motto ! I wouldn't tell him about it for the world, though."

CHAPTER NINE

" SPORTS BEFORE BREAKFAST "

ON TUESDAY evening Julian nipped over the wall to inspect
the remaining fruit.

Most of the raspberries which were left would be fully
ripe by the next day. They could clear the remaining red
currants in the morning.

"We've just about enough baskets," he reported.
"But we've used up the punnets. Are there any bags
about, Miranda ? "

"Look in the kitchen table drawer. There are probably
a few." Rummaging produced a dozen bags.

"We'd better use two for each customer, because the
red currants are so juicy. We can take them out in a
bowl and weigh them there."

They all meant to go to bed earlier on Tuesday, as the
alarm was set for five-thirty. "A quarter of an hour to
get up, five minutes to get ourselves off, and ten minutes
to cycle to the Gardens," Miranda had planned.

By the time Mamie had been lured away from a dustbin
down the road, and Julian had found the back door key,
accidentally kicked into the garden, it was on earlier
than usual.

When the alarm rang the next morning Verna shuddered
and burrowed beneath the bedclothes again.

"Come on," Miranda said grimly. "You can't get out
of it, so you may as well make a start now."

" It's downright cruelty," Verna moaned. " I'm losing my beauty sleep. We should have the right to contract out of such invitations. Jo Ann and Nicky *like* getting up early."

" Come on ! You've accepted the invitation, so you can't back out. By eight o'clock you'll probably be the life and soul of the party."

With more groans Verna got herself, out of bed and, muttering protests to herself, grabbed a tatty but well loved dressing-gown and her slippers, and trailed along to the bathroom.

They all managed to be ready at the appointed time and by then Verna was awake enough to join in the conversation.

The Weavers were waiting at the main gate of the Gardens, each with bags slung over their handle-bars. They seemed to have brought several vacuum flasks each, besides various tins. It was two minutes to six so they stood waiting for Ted Farrow to come and open, which would be on the dot. When he appeared he looked taken aback at the sight of six lively girls and boys with their bicycles.

" You can't ride them through the Gardens," he said ponderously. " It's agin the regulations. You can wheel them, but you can't ride."

" We don't want to ride them," Nicky answered politely. " We're going to padlock them and leave them outside."

This puzzled Ted. At that hour of the day people used the Gardens as a means of getting from one place to another, usually.

" Are you takin' a walk round the Gardens ? " he asked,

eyeing the bulky bags which the Weavers were carrying, and which were surely brought with a purpose.

"We are going to have breakfast here," Nicky said.

"*Breakfast?* All of you?"

"Yes. It's not against the regulations, is it? People bring sandwiches in the dinner hour sometimes in the summer, don't they?"

"Well yes . . . But I've never heard of no one comin' to *breakfast*. You're not allowed on the grass," he added sharply.

"We know that," Giles said. "There are lots of 'Keep off the Grass' notices about. We won't put a foot on it."

"Well, I suppose you can come in," Ted said rather grudgingly. "But don't you leave no litter about."

"It's against the regulations, isn't it?" Verna said innocently. Ted looked at her suspiciously for he felt she might be laughing at him, but her face merely bore an intelligent, inquiring look.

"Yes. Refuse bins are provided."

"Maximum penalty: five pounds for breaking the regulations, isn't it?" Jo Ann put in. "But I don't think they put you into prison." As they went in, Ted looked after them with a puzzled expression. They were up to something, he'd be bound.

The six went to the far end of the Gardens, and on the way, Nicky showed the others the Programme of Events. "We've put down things like two-legged race, and egg and spoon—with potatoes, because we'll all have an equal chance in them. Hundred yards, and high jump were out, because we others would have to have handicaps against Verna and Giles and that's never so satisfactory, as people can never agree as to what handicap each person should have."

Giles began to protest that he didn't need to be given an advantage, but Nicky cut him short. " Egg and spoon ; three-legged ; sack race, then pea and straw—— "

" What's that ? "

" We'll show you. Then we'll have a treasure hunt. Jo Ann will be out of that, because she came in here yesterday afternoon and hid the clues. Then we'll have breakfast. Would anyone like some coffee before we start ? We didn't make tea because coffee tastes nicer from the flask than tea does." Verna was wide awake by now but even she was glad of a cup. The milk, in a separate flask, was piping hot, so the coffee was really good.

Nicky stretched two lengths of string across one of the paths, fifty yards apart. They each had six potatoes which had to be carried past the farther line. " We mustn't get too noisy," he warned them. " If we get Ted's goat up he could order us out, so anyone rowdy will be disqualified."

They all set off in great style, but there were a number of dives after errant potatoes which WOULD fall just when the competitor was near the goal. Verna and Giles nearly collided once but after holding breath while their potatoes wobbled they managed to stay the course. It was touch and go between Jo Ann and Julian, but the girl, over confident, ran the last few yards and sent her sixth potato flying.

" Prize-giving at the end," Nicky said in a business-like way. " Now, how shall we pair up for the three legged ? " Miranda and Jo Ann decided to go together, saying that they did not want their feet to be trodden on by the boys' great clod-hoppers, even though they were all wearing tennis shoes. Verna went with Giles, and as the two of them had practised together a lot in the spring for their respective school Sports Day they easily won.

From the back of the summer-house, hidden in a bush, Nicky produced six old sacks wrapped in an old mac. " I put them there yesterday," he said grinning, " I didn't think there was much risk of them being found."

There was the usual giggling while they got themselves into the sacks. Running and jumping was allowed, and each used the method which seemed best. They were all on their way back, and the excitement made them a little noisy.

" Here comes Ted ! " Verna suddenly cried. Ted was hurrying down the path towards them.

" Don't talk about Regulations any more, or he'll think—we are—being cheeky," Miranda gasped as she bumped along. Just as Nicky had crossed the line, Ted reached them.

" Where did you get those sacks from ? " he cried wrathfully. " Have you been in my shed ? It's strictly forbidden—it's against—— "

" No, we wouldn't dream of going there," Nicky answered. " We brought them ourselves. Look, they're all marked ' L.G.S.', that's my school. I borrowed them from the groundsman."

Ted was partly appeased, but the whole affair seemed to have put him out. Miranda thought he seemed to be trying to think of some Regulation they were breaking, but she knew that they had really been no noisier than the many children who were brought there to play in the afternoons.

" Mr. Farrow," Nicky said persuasively, " I noticed yesterday a most lovely rose over there among the standard roses. It was a sort of coppery red, opening to a silvery pink, and it was scented. The label was faded so I couldn't see the name. Could you tell me what it is ? I'd like to get a standard for my father's birthday."

Nicky did not know it, but as well as Regulations, there was another great passion in Ted Farrow's life, and that was roses. He could not resist discussing them, comparing them, growing and showing them. As it happened, Nicky was not saying this only to change the subject, although he hoped it might. He really had been struck by the beauty of the rose and had hoped he could find out its name.

In spite of himself, the look of annoyance began to fade from Ted's face. " Sounds as if it's Comtesse Vandal," he said gruffly. " Or it could be Mrs. Van Rossem." He hesitated, and looked round to see if they were " having him on " then decided they were not. The subject was irresistible. " Show me which one," he said. " I'll soon tell you." They all trooped over to the roses, which were opening under the early morning sun.

" This is it."

" Ah—that's Comtesse Vandal. No mistaking that : she's a real beauty. Look at that for a rose—— " They stood and admired the lovely show.

" We've got one something like this," Jo Ann said. " This yellow one. Is it McCredy's Yellow ? "

" No, this is a Spek's Yellow, one of the loveliest yellows there is. That's a McCredy, over at the end. You compare the two."

They stood talking for a few moments, Ted pointing

out the beauty of some of his favourites, then he advised Nicky where to go for his rose tree. " Don't get one on the cheap," he said. " Tisn't worth it. Yes, Neasons are the best growers round here." Then he said something about having jobs to do, and stumped off towards his lodge.

" Good ! " Verna said gleefully as they went back to their starting place. " Did you suddenly develop an interest in roses, Nicky, to lead him off the subject ? "

" No I did *not*. It's one thing to pull his leg a bit, but somehow it 'ud seem mean to pretend to be awfully keen on something you weren't really—as if you were laughing to yourself all the time. I know we were making fun of him a bit, at first, but that wasn't the same. I can't explain why." Miranda felt the same way. Ted wasn't a bad old stick, and he'd been quite interesting when he was talking about those fertilisers . . .

The " pea and straw " competition was rather fun. Nobody but Nicky had heard of it. He gave out two saucers, a drinking straw and twenty dried peas to each one. " At the signal, you draw up a pea at a time from the first saucer, and transfer it to the other one," he said. " The first one to move his—or her—twenty peas wins."

" Do you draw the pea *up* the straw ? " Giles asked doubtfully.

" No, idiot ! They're too big to go up. Hold the straw over the pea, just touching. Draw in your breath, and the pea will stay on the end. You have to be quick, or it drops off. I haven't been practising but as I've done it before I'll have five more peas than you."

They sat on the floor of the summer-house, with their two saucers in front of them. Just as they were all bent over their first pea waiting for the signal to start, Julian gave a hoot of laughter. " We look like natives carrying out a tribal ritual," he exclaimed.

" Oh, come *on* ! " Verna hated waiting. " Stop laughing, or you won't be able to draw your breath in."

They laughed over it so much that the peas rolled about in all directions, but finally Jo Ann managed to get her twenty peas on to her second saucer before anyone else. " We've all won an event except you, Miranda," she said. " You *must* get the treasure hunt. That 'ud even things out nicely."

" I can't guarantee to," Miranda said, laughing. " I can't usually find my own things at home, let alone things other people have hidden."

" Well, I've hidden some things in the borders and around here— " Jo Ann indicated the parts they should search in— " and I've put five of each, so you've got a chance to find a set each. There are six articles, and they're all within reach from the paths, or at least, you wouldn't have to go on the grass for anything. Here are the clues of what you are to look for— " she handed them each a folded sheet of paper— " but don't look at them until I say. I'll be here in the summer-house, and the first to bring the six articles to me wins. Ready ? *Go*."

Miranda quickly read the first clue :

" Part of a tree, found in the swimming bath.
  You can make a mat from me, but not a path."

In a swimming bath ? Ropes ? You could make a rope mat, certainly. What was rope made from : fibres, wasn't it ? Hemp. Would you call that part of a tree ? She hesitated, looking around the borders for signs of rope.

Cork floats . . . Cork was part of a tree, and yes, you could get cork mats! She hurried past Giles who was searching round a sundial. She had gone down two paths when she saw it. Ah! there—a small cork, just behind a large pebble! She slipped it into her pocket, and unfolded the paper again. By now Miranda was feeling very keen to win.

" I can make things disappear;
A magic charm? Oh no, not here!
In another shape, I keep you warm,
I can easily change my shape and form."

Humm! What makes things disappear? A bleach? Verna couldn't put bleaches about . . . ink eradicator? They used it at school for blots. But with no stretch of imagination could it keep you warm! She glanced round to see how the others were getting on, and just at that moment Julian gave a shout of: "Eureka!" and pounced on something down by a flower-bed.

There were one or two people going across the Gardens by now, so Miranda did not make her search too obvious, in case a well-meaning passer-by came over to ask if they had lost something. She decided to leave the "disappearing" clue for the time, and looked at the next.

"Five large shillings? Oh, no, no!
But on each pinta one most go."

Was that a mistake, "pinta"? And then in a flash it came to her: An aluminium milk-bottle top. One went on each "pinta" milk! Now to find one! Something glinting by the rockery drew her, and there it was. The next clue said:

> "Fifty little brothers, all in one bed,
>   The brothers are all scattered; bring me one without a head."

Ah—a bed of flowers! Dahlias? There must be at least fifty in that bed. But what did "scattered" mean? Spread about? She was not sure. And why bring one without a head? Jo Ann wouldn't expect them to pick a plant, even if it had no flower on it. She thought back to the second clue again. "I can make things disappear" . . . Oh dear, what could it be? Ah—a *Rubber!* Yes, a hot water bottle keeps you warm, too.

Giles came along, looking from side to side.

"Found any?" she asked.

"Yes, three."

Miranda grimaced. "Only two. Ah!" She pounced on something sticking up next to a petunia plant. "Three, now," she grinned, and went off with the rubber. "Fifty little brothers" . . . it needn't mean flowers . . . did it mean exactly fifty? Something fidgeted the back of her mind; she felt she ought to know it.

Now what was this?

> "A diamond? Not quite,
>   Not nearly so bright;
>   But let's say a cousin.
>   I've planted a dozen."

A "cousin" to a diamond . . . that seemed to ring a

bell. A diamond was a form of carbon, wasn't it? And then—coal was too, wasn't it? Black diamonds, coal used to be called. Got it! The meaning, at least. It was not so easy to find a lump. It was while she was searching for a piece that she found herself staring straight at a nice clean match-stick, without a head. That was it! "Fifty little brothers," in a matchbox at first. That was their bed, and five headless ones were scattered about the garden. Good, she was getting on!

Verna was searching round the base of a little fountain at the junction of two paths as Miranda came along to try another part.

"How are you doing?" Miranda called.

"I've got four. The last one beats me, and the 'disappearing' one—I haven't got a clue! At least, I've got the clue, but I haven't a clue as to what it means."

"I've only got the last one to do. I think I know what to look for, but I can't find it." She suddenly had an idea, and went hurrying off to the summer-house where Jo Ann was sitting reading a magazine. "How many have you found?" she asked, as Miranda burst in. "Five. I'm on my last."

The summer-house was five-sided. Miranda looked quickly into three of the angles formed by the walls, but there was nothing there. The fourth, however, disclosed a small cotton-reel, partly hidden by a dead leaf. She glanced at the last clue again to make sure.

"At making rhymes I'm not expert,
In fact, my head begins to reel.
Now you've only one more clue.
Do you cotton on? You should, I feel."

" If this cotton-reel isn't the answer, I'll eat it for breakfast ! " Miranda cried triumphantly.

" Good ! " Jo Ann exclaimed. " I'll check over your other things . . . yes, you're the winner ! There's still one cotton-reel left, Verna's, I believe. Oh, here comes Julian."

" Just found my sixth ! " he cried.

" Sorry, too late ! Miranda's beaten you by a head."

" Jolly good ! Now we've all won something. Here comes Giles." Verna was last, as it was not until she realised that, as Miranda had been declared winner soon after she had gone into the summer-house, the last clue probably led there.

" The clues were jolly good," Julian declared.

" The verses were not of high literary value ! " Jo Ann acknowledged. " But I hadn't long to do them in. By the way, I put a dozen small pieces of coal about, partly because I wanted a rhyme for ' cousin ', and partly because they're not easy to notice among the pebbles and stones."

" I got the first clue easily, but the coal stumped me for quite a time ! I was trying to think of the name of a plant that might fit in."

" It was the other way with me. I finished up with the first clue. Well now, breakfast, or prizes first ? "

" Breakfast ! " was the chorus, everyone suddenly realising how long it was since supper-time the night before. Jo Ann produced beakers, bowls, plates and forks for everybody.

" Forks ! " Verna exclaimed. " That looks promising."

" Two-course hot breakfast," Jo Ann said with pride. " We didn't see why not. We can't very well fry bacon and eggs here—at least, we could have tried but we

thought Ted might go up in smoke at the idea ! Besides,
Mummy said we weren't to light *anything* in case
of fire. But there's porridge to start with. I know you
don't have porridge much in the summer, but we thought
we'd all be pretty hungry." She opened a wide-mouthed
flask and scooped out a helping for each. It had kept
quite hot, and with the addition of hot milk and sugar was
really enjoyed by all of them. They sat on the summer-
house floor and stacked the empty bowls in a pile. From
a tin Jo Ann produced slices of buttered toast. " Cold,
I'm afraid," she told them, " but this will warm it up."
From another big flask came scrambled egg. " Have it
while it's hot," she urged, putting a good heap on each
slice.

" Funny how food always tastes so much nicer in the
open air than it does at home," Verna remarked, adding
salt and pepper.

" Yes. However did you get all these flasks ? " Julian
asked, as Nicky poured out coffee from one, and then
opened a fresh one of hot milk.

" Oh, we borrowed from friends. The next-doors have
got a super picnic basket, with these food containers, and
ones for thick soup. They're jolly useful. Jo Ann got me
up at five, because we couldn't expect this stuff to keep
really hot if we put it in overnight."

" *Five* o'clock ? Verna thought it was torture when I
routed her out at half past."

They finished up with oranges, and then came the
Grand Prize-Giving, for which the two Weavers had
spent some time going round Woolworth's. There was a
drawing book for Miranda's prize ; the two-legged
winners got ball pens ; Julian's egg and spoon win got him

a pocket comb; Nicky presented his sister solemnly with an address book for the "straw and pea" competition, while he got a scrap book for his sack race.

"Remember the knitting competition we had before we moved, Nicky?" Jo Ann suddenly asked.

"Rather!" her brother said, grinning. The others wanted to know about it, so Jo Ann told them.

"The English mistress at my last school was awfully keen on working for the displaced persons camps, and she would give us ounce balls of double knitting wool, and get us to make squares to join together for blankets. After we had made a number we slacked off a bit—it was rather boring—so one of the second form girls had an idea. There was a jolly good film on, a comedy, in the Easter Holidays, so Deborah suggested that about a dozen of us should go one afternoon and have a knitting party. We would take a new ounce ball each, and our needles, and whoever used up the most wool during the film, got a prize. Oh, we were allowed to cast on the stitches before we went in. We paid sixpence entrance fee to her, and that went to the funds."

"Why does Nicky remember it?"

"Because," he answered, "it sounded amusing, so I thought it would be fun to enter too, if they would let me. Jo Ann taught me plain knitting, but I was no expert, especially in the dark, so my effort looked more like an an egg cosy."

"I bet it did! Who won?"

"I forget, but I didn't!" Jo Ann admitted. "The film was so funny that I laughed until I nearly fell off my seat, and I kept dropping my knitting and the stitches kept falling off. But it was great fun. Although the film was a bit noisy, the clicking of our knitting needles could be heard now and then, and an old gentleman a few rows in front kept looking round. I believe he thought there was a time bomb ticking away, and due to go off at any moment. I wonder they didn't turn us out ! "

They cleared up before they left the gardens, and Giles was sent to put paper bags, six straws and a hundred and twenty dried peas into the refuse bin. On the way he tripped, and the peas shot into a flower-bed. " I grabbed up all I could see," he reported ruefully, " but there are a lot still there. If they come up next spring Ted will think he's got a new variety of plant. I think I'll come along and see, about next April. I know—I'll tell him they look like ' driedeopolis peapolis,' very rare, and that Kew Gardens would like a specimen."

" *Very* clever ! " said Julian. " We can take some of those things in our carriers, Nicky," and they went out of the gates.

CHAPTER TEN

CRISIS OVER

IT WAS just the morning for a cycle ride. The sun was warm, but there was a slight breeze. They set off for Chippenham Valley, riding two abreast, and singing as they went.

It was a favourite ride with them all for there were some miles of level road, then a spin down for two miles into the Valley, and not much uphill work the rest of the way back.

They arrived at Weaver's Cottage *starving*, according to Nicky.

"Just as I expected," said Mrs. Weaver. "Coffee and sandwiches are nearly ready."

Pleasant as it was to sit in the garden under the willow trees, the Harveys did not linger. By eleven they were in Mr. Blake's garden, searching for the last of the fruit.

They soon picked nine pounds of raspberries and two of currants.

"There won't be many left by Friday," Miranda remarked. "I say—let's give the Merricks a jar of jam for letting us use the trailer."

"Good idea. And I must give his bike a good clean, and scrub out the trailer."

They could not face a meal at midday so, although Miranda had resolved not to let meals get out of hand while Dad was away, she felt that this week she would have to compromise a bit. They loaded the trailer, and on the way to Emm's she bought meat pies and doughnuts to eat out, resolving to cook when they got back for high tea.

Business was slack—until the Junior who was such a "fan" of Miranda's came along.

"Hallo," she exclaimed. "I came yesterday but you weren't here." They explained why.

"You've still got lots of jam to sell," Mavis remarked. "I've no pocket-money, or I'd buy some. I'm calling round to three addresses for things for the Church Fête Grocery Stall."

An hour went by, and three baskets and seven jars changed hands.

"Twenty one jars left," said Giles. "Twenty, without the Merricks'."

"Yes—that's what's bothering me."

They sat just inside Emm's gate eating their lunch when Mavis cycled up. She nearly fell off her bicycle with excitement.

"What do you think?" she cried, "Old Mrs. Garfield said that she and her housekeeper had both been down with 'flu, so they hadn't bought anything for the stall, but she gave me a pound and asked me to give it to the stall-holder."

"Jolly good of her."

"Yes, but listen! I suddenly thought of your jam, and I asked if she would like me to buy some for the stall. She thought it was a good idea, and she gave me two more shillings, so that I could buy twelve jars."

"Mavis, you *darling!*"

Mavis went bright pink, then held out the money.

"I'll deliver them," Giles offered. "Where do you want them taken?"

He made a couple of journeys with her and when he got back, found Miranda looking pleased. "Everything's sold but six jars," she said with satisfaction. "And here come the others to relieve us. They're not to *dare* come home until they've sold out."

By mid-afternoon Verna and Julian arrived back, jubilant.

"Got rid of the lot! I'm going up with the trailer when I've cleaned it up. Where's the jar of jam?"

Later, there was a hilarious high-tea—a fry-up of all the girls could lay hands on. Julian had brought back an ice cream block and everybody felt that it was in the nature of a celebration. It had been quite fun, but the fact that the fruit had got to be sold once it was picked rather took the novelty off.

After everything was washed up Julian got out his account book and laid the money on the table. After totting up he announced: "Eleven pounds twelve shillings and tenpence—that's what we should have after expenses are deducted. That's better than a tonic, any day, I should think." He counted the money, and to everyone's secret relief it was exactly right.

They decided to keep the money until they knew Mr. Blake was back, rather than risk dropping it into the letter-box of an empty house.

Verna fingered the piles of silver. "Isn't it maddening! To think that we've earned all this for Mr. Blake and yet our five pounds had to go for the Northwoods' fencing!"

"That's life, my child!" Julian answered. "Let us face life in all its reality, as the poet Wordsworth would doubtless have said, if I hadn't thought of it first."

"And don't speak of that five pound note," Miranda

begged. " Because nobody has thought of any way of making money. Or have they ? " There was dead silence. " Oh well, no harm in asking."

They drew up a letter to put in with the money. After much pencil chewing they produced this between them :—

" Mr. Blake.
Dear Sir,

We were sorry to hear of your accident and hope that you are better.

We realised that your soft fruit would rot if it was not picked while you were in hospital, so we picked it and marketed it for you.

We enclose eleven pounds twelve shillings and ten pence. We sold some as jam to prevent some of the fruit from going bad. We also enclose an account of expenses which amounted to thirteen shillings and two pence.

We apologise for breaking and entering, but as our father is away we had to use our own judgment.

Miranda, Julian, Verna and Giles Harvey.

It was very pleasant to get a phone call the next morning from a friend of Miranda's asking them all over for the day. At first the boys were distinctly unappreciative.

" Ruth Charlton ? Isn't that the girl who said she *liked* learning French verbs, when she came to tea ? " inquired Julian in disgust. " And raving about poetry, and quoting Scott : 'Breathes there a man with soul so dead——' "

" That's Tennyson," Verna interrupted.

" *Scott*."

" It's not. It's *Tennyson*," shouted Verna determinedly.

There was a dash to the bookcase where well worn books, so often used that they never got that musty smell, dwelt in happy disarray. There was a triumphant shout from Julian.

" There ! Look at that ! And I wouldn't dream of saying ' I told you so.'—I'm much too well-bred for that."

" Oh well, I wasn't far out," Verna said, unabashed. " They're next to each other in the alphabet."

" I don't have to go, do I ? " Giles asked. " I was going to clean my bike."

" Don't bother, then. You boys would probably find it dull. And I don't suppose you'd be able to follow the conversation," Miranda said calmly, " since there'll only be Ruth and her parents, and her uncle who is one of the top men at the Atomic Research Station, and her cousin, who went on the Schoolboys' Scientific Expedition to Iceland. We'll manage without you—— "

" *What ! Who* did you say ? "

" Not *Stephen Charlton ?* Would he be Ruth's uncle ? "

" Yes," Miranda answered carelessly. " You boys can clean your bikes to your hearts' content and I'll leave a fish pie and bread pudding ready for you."

" Don't be a BEAST. She's quite nice, really ! Only she did seem a bit of a swot."

" Well, I'll tell her to talk to you in words of one syllable, then. So we're all going ? "

They had a wonderful day. Stephen Charlton promised to get them some autographs of quite famous people, and his son Roger told some amusing anecdotes about the

Expedition and made Iceland seem a real country, and
not just a place on the map. Ruth seemed to have forgotten French verbs and talked incessantly about the
latest pop singers.

" It just shows how mistaken you can be about people,"
Julian remarked thoughtfully when they got back.

" Too true ! They probably expected us to bring two
little brothers with grubby knees who talked of nothing
but comics and toffee apples, and instead they found you
both reasonably intelligent," Miranda teased.

The next morning the girls felt they really must give
the place a good turn out. Giles got out the vacuum
cleaner and Julian did the stairs.

" I say," Verna called from the landing window, where
she was shaking out a duster. " The Northwoods are
back. I can see Mrs. Northwood at the french windows.
I thought I heard their car drive up a few minutes ago.
They must have come home earlier than they expected."

" I wonder if they have found the letter yet ! *And*
that five pound note. I feel so annoyed about it."

While Miranda was polishing the landing and Verna
was cleaning the inside of the bedroom window the phone
rang. Giles answered it. The next moment he came
bounding up the stairs. " It's Mr. Northwood," he said.
" He wants to know if we can go round to see him for a
few minutes."

" Oh horrors ! Did he sound mad ? "

" No, he just sounded ordinary. Like an old man
usually does over the phone, I should say."

" Perhaps he's furious. Perhaps he wants to wipe the
floor with the lot of us."

" Well, he's got that five pound note of ours—— "

" If anyone mentions that five pound note again I think I shall scream," Miranda declared with feeling.

" He's waiting for an answer."

" Oh, tell him we'll be over in ten minutes, if that will suit him." The boys grumbled a bit, as it meant getting out of torn shorts into something more respectable, but five minutes later they were standing on their neighbours' doorstep.

" Ah, come in," the white-haired gentleman exclaimed.

" We are so sorry about the fence," Miranda began, feeling that they ought to start off.

" That's what we wanted to see you about. Ah—here's my wife." The next moment they were sitting in the pleasant room leading into the garden. From where they sat, no one could see the unfortunate gap in the fence . . .

" Now, we found your envelope when we returned this morning. We came back earlier than we intended, because I have an important engagement unexpectedly for to-morrow."

" We hope it won't be much of a bother, to have the fence repaired."

" Oh, an accident can happen to everybody. It was good of you to take the responsibility, all of you. It must have been worrying, especially as your father is away. Fortunately, we are covered by insurance, so we can put in a claim—— "

" *Insurance !* "

" Why, I never thought of that ! "

" Does that mean we don't have to pay ? "

Mrs. and Mr. Northwood could not help smiling at the four startled faces in front of them.

"Well, weren't we mutts not to think of that!" Julian exclaimed.

"I do know that if you are insured and you have a fire the insurance people will pay for it, but it didn't occur to me that if you burn anyone else's property they would pay for it," Miranda said joyfully.

"You poor things!" Mrs. Northwood murmured. "Now you needn't worry any more."

Mr. Northwood picked the envelope up from the table. "Your five pound note—oh, and the sixpence," he said with a twinkle.

"I think you were very clever to work out how much it should cost," his wife put in. "Sums like that are too much for me! My answer would probably have run into hundreds of pounds!"

"Saint Christopher will be glad to get it back," Giles said with great satisfaction.

"Saint Christopher?" Mr. Northwood looked politely interrogative, and Giles explained.

"Well, I'm glad we are not depriving the good saint of his guardianship," the old gentleman said kindly. "I'll get on to the Insurance people to-day, and before long the fence will be better than ever. Although I don't advise you to repeat the process!"

It seemed like a dream when the four found themselves back in their own hall, with Julian getting down the picture, and Giles fetching the roll of sellotape.

"That really is a load off my mind!" Miranda remarked, as she fixed the note back into place. "There —I'm sure Saint Christopher looks pleased."

CHAPTER ELEVEN

A SHOCK FOR VERNA

" I wonder if Mr. Blake is coming back to-morrow," Verna remarked as they were returning from a cricket match that evening.

"Quite likely. Oh Verna, did you take back that catalogue you picked up by accident with the baskets the other day ? It ought to go back to Mr. Blake's shed. I saw it on the dresser."

" Gosh ! I forgot it. I'll slip over with it when we get home ; you won't see me putting my foot on Blake territory after to-day."

It was beautifully cool when Verna strolled into the garden after they had eaten. It was wonderful to have the holidays and there was enough left for the end not to be in sight . . . she wondered what Dad was doing. How-ever they were enjoying themselves there was always a gap in the family, like a missing tooth. After to-day there would be no more rushing off to Emm's—although Verna had a quiet glow of satisfaction at the thought of an undertaking carried through.

She slipped over the wall and took a last look at the raspberry canes. Here and there she could see a solitary berry, a great sultry red globule of sweetness, hanging among the dark leaves ; there were just enough for a man not long out of hospital to be able to pick a bowlful for several breakfasts . . .

She made her way down to the shed and wriggled

through the window, put the catalogue back on the bench and then had a look round to make sure that the shed was left just as they had found it. Out once again, she pushed the window back into place.

It was very quiet except for the bird song. There were a number of trees in the garden and so it looked bigger than it was. Verna got back to the raspberries, and one particularly large one caught her eye. It was too tempting. As she bent down to pick it, an ice-cold voice from a few yards down the path said :

" I hope you enjoyed all the other raspberries—there must have been plenty even for the four of you ! Don't let me stop you : there are a few left over here."

Verna stood frozen. The sudden voice in the quiet garden would have startled her in any case, but the bitter scorn in Mr. Blake's voice paralysed her.

The three others were listening to a quiz programme when suddenly Verna burst in upon them.

" He's back— " she said, her eyes blazing. " He's back, and he thinks we came over and stole his fruit."

" Who ? Mr. Blake ? "

" Yes—he told me not to bo-bother about him, but to go on and pick the lot ! I—I couldn't think what to say. I just couldn't answer him. I—I just stood there, with him looking at me. Then I b-bolted over the wall again. Oh, it was horrid ! "

She was choking back the tears but they would come. Miranda knew that her sister, like all the Harveys, hated to be seen crying. " It must have startled you to find him standing there," she said. " It'ud upset anyone."

" It's not just that ! " Verna retorted. " It's because I'm

furious. We've worked hard to look after his affairs just because he was helpless, and we had all that job over j-j-jam," her voice trembled, " and getting soaked through, and then we're blamed ! He didn't give me a ch-chance to explain. We were being good neighbours, and he practically called us thieves ! And I just stood there like an idiot. I feel *mad* with him and with myself. I just couldn't think where to start ! "

" Here, sit down." Julian gave her a kindly shove into the old leather chair which, through long practice, was able to adjust itself to everybody's shape. " It must have been beastly for you. It always is when our good intentions are . . . what's it ? . . . misinterpreted. It was like that at school when I tried to help old Stinks open a tin that had stuck, and shot a lot of green powder over his hair. He was *not* appreciative."

Julian's easy conversation helped to steady Verna, and she gave a wan smile.

" You know," Miranda said thoughtfully, " I suppose it was only natural for him to think that we had nipped over and nicked his fruit. It would seem a mean thing to do when he was in hospital."

" Yes," agreed Julian. " He may have only just got back, and have strolled into the garden to have a look round. He'd expect to find some of the fruit spoiled, but not the canes practically stripped. I *wish* we had put the money in his letter-box the other day, even if it was a risk."

" We're proper juvenile delinquents now, in his opinion."

" What shall we do ? "

" Suppose we all go and explain ? "

" I'm not going near him ! " Verna gave a convulsive sob. She knew that it was partly self-pity which had upset her. At school, where she was often in hot water, she cheerfully put up with impositions, detention, lost marks and even being sent to the Head if she felt she deserved it, but if she was blamed or punished for what was not her fault, it made her furious.

Giles had been silent up till now. " I'll go and explain, if you like," he said. "After all, he'll have to listen—he can't sling me out because of hurting his ribs."

Miranda did not want another awkward interview. It might permanently fix the breach between the two sides if anyone spoke too hastily. "Let's write *another* letter explaining, and pin it on to the envelope with the first letter and the money, and put it in his letter-box with Julian's account book. He can't think then that we're just making it up."

They all felt that that was the best thing to do, but it was with a curiously flat feeling that each tried to draft something out. They had not felt nearly so bad over the letter to Mr. Northwood, although they had known that he could have been justifiably annoyed with them.

After some arguing, Julian and Miranda took the best bits from each one's efforts, and produced this :

" Dear Mr. Blake,
    We think the enclosed letter etc. will explain just what we have been doing, better than we can.
    It is understandable that you should have jumped to conclusions when you saw Verna in your garden. She had been returning a catalogue which had been accidently taken away from the shed.

We hope that you will put down our actions to an attempt to be neighbourly, and not to interference.

Hoping that you are now recovered.

> Yours truly,
> Miranda, Julian, Verna and Giles Harvey."

"It seems to be rather more friendly than we meant," Miranda said, as she signed it. "Oh well, it's nine o'clock now, and time you were in bed, Giles. If you're going to take the letter round you'd better go now."

Giles had only got to the front gate when there was an urgent call from Julian. "Give me that account book for a moment—I want to check up . . . Yes! I suddenly remembered that I was doodling the other day when I had the book out—if Mr. Blake saw this he wouldn't be too edified." Round the page which showed the first day's takings was inscribed "Mr. Simple Simon Blake" half a dozen times in various styles of handwriting. On the page showing the last entry "Mr. Simple Simon" was asking the pieman for a pie, and holding out a cheque for eleven pounds, twelve shillings and tenpence. The next picture showed a huge crate, labelled "Raspberry pies" and addressed to Mr. Simple Simon Blake, being delivered to Bat Tree Cottage.

"Glory! I'll have to tear these pages out and do them again, minus embellishments. I'll only be a few minutes, Giles."

"It would serve him right if he'd seen them," Giles protested, examining the drawings critically, but a short time later he took the book containing a censured version of the accounts, and the fat envelope with the new letter attached round to Bay Tree Cottage.

Giles was not easily abashed but even he went up their neighbour's path rather gingerly, dropped the things in the letter-box and scampered down the path again.

"Let's do something different to-morrow to help us to forget all this bother," Miranda said when he got back, with Mamie in his arms. "I had a brain-wave just now—you know how shabby Dad's bedroom walls are. They haven't been done for some time. If we can raise the cash between us, let's distemper them for a surprise for him when he comes back. Those plastic emulsion paints are jolly good, because you can scrub them. Then, if any more tomato soup was splashed it wouldn't matter." That was a reference to one of the rare times when Dad had had a couple of days in bed, with a frightful cold, and Miranda had slipped on a mat and had shot across the bedroom with a bowl of soup—it *would* be bright orange, instead of that greyish mushroom—and had left a series of streaks in a conspicuous spot.

Everyone cheered up.

"What colour shall we do it?"

"He did say once that he had rather a hankering after a nice sunshine yellow to help him face the day, especially when his bank balance was rather low."

"Let's start directly after breakfast." Verna was quite cheered up by now. "Don't let's spend hours washing down, and all that fiddling about. I like to see a transformation taking place in front of my eyes."

"We'll have to do some preliminary work, but we'll keep it to the minimum." The truth was that they were all impatient to get to the exciting part instead of filling in every little crack.

"I believe the Weavers have a roller. I'll go round first

thing and borrow it, and you girls can get the paint," and Julian went off to mark another day off the calendar.

In a burst of energy Miranda got up at six and began heaving things about in her father's bedroom. She put down dust sheets and gave the walls a good brush down, working quietly so as not to disturb Miss Hodges above.

They collected about fifteen shillings between them, and Julian agreed to pay out a little pocket money in advance, if necessary. It was surprising how soon things got moving. By nine the girls were in the village hardware shop. They could not get the shade they wanted so they bought two shades to mix together, and a small tin of white.

" Gosh ! this is a vicious shade of yellow ! " Julian exclaimed as he stirred up one tin. " Dad will think he's going up in smoke—you can nearly smell the sulphur."

" Don't worry ! You wait until I put this primrose in, and some of the white. You're to put on your oldest clothes, all of you, because this stuff doesn't wash out."

They looked like scarecrows when they were ready to begin. The bucket of distemper looked wonderful, and when Miranda tried it out on a sample strip it was as near sunshine yellow as anyone could want.

" Gorgeous ! " Verna exclaimed. " It'll make those curtains look sorry for themselves—and the bedspread." The " soft furnishings " had faded and washed out to a very pale blue. After some deliberation the girls decided to bleach the remaining colour out, and perhaps dye them. Miranda left Julian to start the walls while she snatched up curtains and bedspread and carried them off to wash.

They each took a turn with the roller and by ten o'clock,

when there was a ring at the door, they were all rather splashed with distemper and, according to Julian, "radiating sunshine for all they were worth."

"That will be the laundry man with the sheets," Miranda decided. "Giles, my little sunbeam, go and take them in, will you? The purse is just behind the tea caddy."

"Anything to keep that sunny smile on your face, my little fairy queen! And, by the way, you've got a blond streak on the front of your hair—very fashionable! You look like the girl at the bacon counter, only she's got mauve lips to go with hers."

"Go *on*! or he won't wait."

Giles went leaping down the stairs two at a time. After a minute or two he came running up in a more subdued way.

"It's Mr. Blake," he said. "He says, can he speak to us all for a few minutes. I've shown him into the sitting-room."

"Mr. Blake! Oh gosh, look at us!"

"Just *look* at my arms—I'm yellow up to my elbows."

"What kind of mood is he in?"

"He looks a bit nervous," Giles declared. "And he looks different. He isn't in those sloppy old clothes he usually wears. But buck up—we can't keep him waiting while we all have baths."

Miranda got agitated and kept ineffectually patting her hair; Verna pulled off her big overall and went to put her arms under the tap in the bathroom; Julian threw off the flowered pinny which he had put on in spite of the jeers of his brother, while Giles seemed quite unperturbed. The fact was, all of them except Giles, felt awkward at meeting this neighbour who had lived in the house over the wall for nearly two years, and who, for most of that time had looked through them when he met them.

"Come on," Julian said. "Let's run our face flannels over our faces and hands and leave it at that. If we stop to change and spruce up he may think we're keeping him waiting on purpose."

So in their oldest jeans, shirts, shorts and assorted gym shoes and casuals they trailed down to the sitting-room, their hands only just dry.

Mr. Blake was standing by the fireplace looking at a pinned up version of "Bill Bailey," written and illustrated by Verna, and starting : " Won't you come home, Dad Harvey, won't you come home ? "

He turned as they came in, swallowed, and said, " I . . . er . . . "

"Won't you sit down ? " Miranda said in her best Aunt Eleanor manner. "Are you feeling better ? "

"Better ! " Mr. Blake suddenly came to life. "Better ! I feel a worm—less important than a worm, really, because a worm does at least some good in a garden ! And now, when other people have been doing work in MY garden, all I do us to accuse them of stealing ! " Mr. Blake was walking backwards and forwards across the sitting-room, and glaring—"like a caged lion," Julian thought to himself, then decided that that was too obvious a simile.

"I expect it did seem suspicious," Julian said.

"And I should really have stopped and explained," Verna added, suddenly finding it easy to talk to their neighbour.

"But I didn't give you the chance. I began making some of my famous sarcastic remarks—no wonder you didn't stop to hear any more. I ought to have realised that you were not that sort of children . . . and then I found your letter and the money in the letter-box, and knew that you had risked a snub and done all that for me, well, I just don't know what to say."

"Wouldn't it be simplest," came Giles's clear voice, "just to say that you are sorry, and come and sit down ? "

Mr. Blake turned and looked at him as if he had never seen him before.

"Why yes—I suppose it would be ! Look, I ought to have taken your word about Laddie "— he looked towards Julian—" because I had never found you out in a lie. But I was so furious when I saw Laddie's cut that I went for the nearest person. When I cooled down I wished I hadn't accused you of throwing the stone, but my stupid pride wouldn't let me say I could have been mistaken. I'm sorry."

"That's all right," Julian said quickly.

"And then," Mr. Blake turned to Verna, "when I saw you in the garden yesterday, I jumped to conclusions and blamed you. Well, I'm sorry about that, and for treating all of you like strangers whenever we met. I've been an idiot ! "

"We're all idiots, sometimes," Julian and Verna said in exactly the same breath, almost as if they had rehearsed it, and that made them all laugh.

"That's all right, then," Verna said quite happily. "I'm glad we all feel better. It's horrid not being friendly with neighbours."

"This is a comfortable chair." Giles dragged one forward. Mr. Blake lowered himself into the old leather arm-chair. "And now that I've got that off my chest," he said, " I can say a very big ' thank you ' to you all for picking my fruit and selling it for me. And for making the jam—— "

" We'll feel more like neighbours when you have eaten our salt," remarked Miranda. " At least, not salt really, but I expect you know what I mean. Cake and coffee, or lemonade would make a good substitute, I think."

Mr. Blake said that he would love a cup of coffee to pull him round. " I felt," he confessed, "when I was coming over here, just as I used to feel at school when I had to go before the headmaster because of some misdeed, only this time there were two headmasters and two headmistresses—at least, that's what it felt like."

The girls went into the kitchen and in a few minutes, coffee for four and lemonade for one were on the way.

" I'm glad we bought a cake this morning," Miranda remarked as she deftly strained the coffee into a jug. " Get it out, will you ? Then there's only the milk to heat."

As they came into the sitting-room they heard Giles say : " You'd better begin calling us by our names, because we'll be calling to you from our side now, when we see you in your garden."

" Right, Giles." Mr. Blake was evidently still feeling a little shy.

Over coffee and ginger cake they soon forgot any embarrassment. Mr. Blake wanted to know about all that had happened since his accident. He had no idea that they had telephoned the hospital. " I was badly concussed," he told them, " and they are always very careful with that in hospital, because if you aren't kept very quiet you can be left with recurrent headaches."

"We could tell that you were meaning to market the fruit, because of all those baskets in the shed. Weren't you worried about all that fruit being left to rot?"

"I was, when I was able to think at all! When they got me to hospital and I found I'd be there a week or so, I got someone to write to a cousin of mine who lives twenty miles from here. I said that if he liked to go over and pick the fruit he could have the lot. You know, my head was so bad I just couldn't think of the names of the shops I sold the raspberries to last year. I couldn't even remember the name of the town! So I thought my cousin might as well benefit."

Miranda thought how strange it was to see Mr. Blake sitting comfortably with his legs crossed, munching a large piece of cake and drinking his second cup of coffee. And then she had an awful thought. "Did your cousin come over, and find we'd picked the fruit?" she asked.

"No—" she heaved a sigh of relief— "There was a letter waiting for me when I got back yesterday evening. He said that they were away on holiday when the letter from the hospital came, and he didn't get it until a day or two ago, when his sister, who came in to air the place for them forwarded it. He said he won't be back until to-morrow, so I knew it wasn't HE who had stripped the canes!"

Mamie came in just then and was introduced. She graciously accepted a piece of cake and settled herself under Giles's chair.

"Now tell me, how did you get the idea of marketing the fruit?" Between the four of them they told him their plan and how it had developed. Verna told him about Mrs. Bostock's sister Emm, while Miranda related how the old chap whom they always referred to as " man and boy " took a poor view of their stall.

Soon Mr. Blake had heard a full account. When Miranda told him why they had made the jam, he looked thoughtful. " It can't exactly have been a picnic for you," he remarked. " It's one thing to do a job just for fun, but it's another thing to feel you've got to keep on with it. I really am grateful to you for coming to the rescue, and the eleven pounds twelve and tenpence was a wonderful surprise. We must celebrate later on, when I'm quite fit again."

Just then Miranda caught sight of the yellow streaks which decorated Verna's forehead and which had escaped the face flannel.

" Oh dear ! " she exclaimed, " We must look AWFUL ! You caught us just about at our worst. Whatever did you think of the lot of us when we came in ? " Looking round at the three others, she wondered what on earth Aunt Eleanor would have thought of them.

" Well, I did think you might all be suffering from a mild attack of yellow jaundice ! " their visitor said with a wry smile. " But it's nothing to what I look like when I'm doing a ceiling ! " They told him that it was walls, and that they would like to show him the bedroom when it was finished.

" I should like to see it in all its glory," he replied. " I say—I'm afraid I've been sitting on some letters, or something." He pulled a few sheets of paper which were sticking up from the side of the chair cushion. As he held them out to Julian who was sitting next to him, by chance he caught sight of something written on the top sheet.

" Blake— " he said, and then stopped. Julian went

scarlet because there was no use trying to pretend, out of politeness, that " Mr Simple Simon Blake " referred to someone else, and not to the startled man who was looking at it.

" I'm frightfully sorry— " Julian stammered. " I was just . . . it was only . . . when I'm doodling I don't really think of what I'm doing."

Having seen so much, Mr. Blake found his eyes drawn to the drawing below. In a moment a smile spread along his lips, and he looked up with a twinkle. " May I see the rest ? " he asked. " It's supposed to be good for us to see ourselves as others see us."

Julian could only hold out the leaves torn from his account book. In a moment Mr Blake began to laugh, and to Julian's relief everyone began to join in.

" I'll keep them, if I may," ' Simple Simon ' declared, " then if ever I'm suffering from a swelled head, I shall only need to look at this to be cured. And now I had better leave you to go on with your sunshine transformation scene, but I'll be calling over the wall to you before long, and then we must start to make merry. Oh—when is your father due back ? "

They told him, and he said if they would put in a good word for him when their father was home, he would make his peace with him.

He thanked Miranda for the " elevenses," and they all saw him to the front door. He went off in quite a jaunty fashion, looking very different to the embarrassed creature who had been shown in.

" I think he's *nice !* " Verna said in her usual generous, impulsive fashion. " And to think we've wasted all this time, on both sides of the fence, hating each other ! "

CHAPTER TWELVE

INTERIOR DECORATORS

THAT AFTERNOON the decorating progressed at a great rate.

"Gleaming white paint would look lovely with this yellow," Verna suddenly said. "Do you think we could rise to it?" The others thought that by drawing some pocket money in advance they could buy white enamel paint, so Giles was sent down to the hardware shop.

"It's a shame to put back these faded curtains and bedspread." Miranda had that look in her eye that meant she had an idea, and didn't mean to be put off it.

"You don't propose that we should buy curtains and a bedspread, do you?" inquired Julian. "Because that would need some doing."

"No. But we could bleach them and dye them . . . I'd hate them to go streaky, though."

Directly Giles got back they all set to. Tea was a quick snack, and by seven o'clock it was finished.

"There!" said Julian. "Dad will think he's in a first-class cabin in the Queen Elizabeth when he wakes up to this!"

As they sat down to sardines on toast Miss Hodges came in and trudged up to her room. Soon a series of thumps could be heard from up above.

"I think she's doing ' keep fit ' exercises up there with a punch ball," Verna exclaimed.

By the morning the paint was dry. What a transformation! Julian cast a critical glance round. "Good! It'll be nice to potter about next week."

"Verna and I will be pottering round the wash-tub," Miranda said grimly. "We're going to turn the soft furnishings into something that doesn't resemble dust sheets so much."

"Here's Miss Hodges—let's show her."

Miss Hodges looked round appreciatively. "It *does* look nice!" she said. "The soft yellow goes well with the mushroom carpet."

"The carpet's rather shabby; it used to be in the sitting-room."

"It was brought up here," Giles explained, "because a bottle of indian ink was tipped over it and wouldn't come out. We were all making Christmas cards, and when the bell rang, we all rushed—we were expecting Uncle John —" Julian tried to catch his eye. Giles would go on and on! "—and when we came back there was a black pool. The stain comes under the bed, so it doesn't show."

Miranda told Miss Hodges about their plans for dyeing. "We'd need a big container," she said doubtfully. "I should think it wouldn't take much to make it come out in streaks and blotches, as if it had a kind of horrible fabric skin disease."

"We could say it's the new fashion in art," Giles said hopefully.

"Couldn't you girls do some sewing—you, know, embroidery, on the curtains and cover?" Julian suggested. There were screams of protest from his sisters, who insinuated that this was comparable to making the Bayeaux Tapestry.

" Have you done any fabric printing ? " Miss Hodges inquired.

" We were going to at school, but we've had several changes of art mistresses, and each one started a new syllabus."

" How would you like to print a repeat pattern in washable colour ? I do a lot of printing as a hobby, and I could show you, if you like."

They all thought this a wonderful idea.

" I print with lino or wood blocks," Miss Hodges went on. " I finished some curtaining last night. You may have heard me—— "

" Oh, was it the banging ? "   Miranda caught Giles's eye and fixed it with an expression which said, don't you dare tell her all the things we pretended it might be.

" I hope I didn't disturb you."

They assured her it didn't matter in the least.

" Then perhaps you would like to experiment a little to-day. I'll give you some bits of lino, and lend you my cutting tools."

She went upstairs and soon came back with her arms full of equipment. She quickly cut a design, rolled some fabric ink on to the block, rolled it over the lino, then took a " pull," as she called it.

" There," she said, " you've got the idea ? Suppose you all make up a design. We could choose the best."

When Miss Hodges had gone they all tried their hands at designing.

" Let's each have a proper turn with the tools and the roller and things, take a print, then make way for the next one, instead of all working at the same time, with someone breathing down one's neck while they're waiting for the roller, and making rude remarks about other people's work."

"That sentence sounds slightly involved in its grammar, brother. I wouldn't like to have to analyse it."

"Well—you know what I mean. Don't let's—or, let's not, if you'd rather—look at each other's designs."

"Right. Our own undiluted genius! Verna and I had better have a go first, or we'll never get a meal. I'm going to make an apricot tart."

Miranda did not take long over her effort, and the table was clear for her sister. Verna sighed and muttered; scrapped one piece of lino, tried another, then seemed fairly satisfied with the print.

Julian spent quite a time, and Sunday dinner was ready before Giles had had his turn. He wanted the meal put off, but the girls were adamant.

"We can't leave the veg. cooking away until all the vitamins have fled," Miranda declared. "There'll be plenty of time this afternoon."

Giles grumbled away through most of the meal, which was rather unlike him. When he did settle down at the sitting-room table he began jabbing away vigorously with the tool until he cut himself, then settled down more cautiously.

The others were out in the garden having a knock-up game of tennis—singles, with the odd one being ball boy and umpire. As Giles came out to say he had finished they heard a "Hi!" from over the wall. There was Mr. Blake, obviously perched on a rather wobbly box. He looked a little shy as if he hadn't yet got used to this "enemies into friends" idea, but Verna called: "Oh, hallo Mr. Blake!

Isn't it nice that we can call over to each other now ! How are you feeling ? "

" Fine, thank you ! By the way, I saw an ice cream man pedalling past just now, so I bought a family brick. As I've no family, I thought you might take pity on me."

They said they would be delighted to, so Giles ran to the shed for the box which they used to put on their side, when they were bringing the raspberries over. Soon they were sitting on the little lawn just outside Mr. Blake's kitchen window.

" I'm afraid the dishes and spoons don't match each other," he remarked. " I haven't got down to the niceties of life yet ! But I've just been commissioned to write a series of short stories for a magazine. I sold one a few weeks ago, and they want more, each with the same central character, so if they are successful, I'll be able to branch out a bit. The money you earned for me was a tremendous help. If I'd come back to find the fruit eaten by the birds, and the rest mouldy under the bushes, it would have been a blow ! "

The others made suitable murmurs. " I'm glad he didn't offer to pay us for the fruit-picking," Miranda thought. " That would have spoiled it all."

They told him about the printing they were going to do, and asked if he would like to see the prints they had just done.

" We haven't seen each others, yet," Julian told him. " You could tell us which you think is the best, then we could see if Miss Hodges agrees."

" No thanks ! " laughed Mr. Blake. " I'm not much of a judge of that sort of thing, and I might drop a clanger ! I'd rather wait and see the work when it's finished."

It was pleasant seeing their neighbour's garden from another view. When the family brick was finished Verna offered to wash up the dishes and spoons. "Oh, don't bother," Mr. Blake said hastily. "I can do it."

"You ought to let us, really!" Verna exclaimed. "You are not quite fit yet, and you look rather pale. Do let me do them." She had swung over so far to Mr. Blake's side that nothing was too good for him, in her eyes. She collected up the things and went towards the kitchen door. "May I go in?" she said politely. Mr. Blake gave a helpless look and muttered something about it not being very tidy.

That was an understatement. In the sink were two burnt saucepans in soak; on the draining-board was a pile of crockery, and a few knives and spoons for good measure.

"It *is* in a bit of a mess," he said apologetically. "I usually have one wash up in the evening, but I'm afraid that I've left it since I've been back. I get tired easily, and then I got down to a bit of writing——" He looked so like Giles trying to justify himself over something he really felt was his fault, that Verna had to laugh. Miranda following in behind said, "You go and rest in the garden again. We'll soon get rid of these if you will give us a tea towel." With some difficulty one was found, and the culprit thankfully retreated.

"Honestly!" Miranda said. "Aren't they all alike?"

"We ought to find him a wife," Verna said decidedly, looking round for the washing-up bowl. "A nice domesticated one who will run the place like clockwork while he gets on with his writing. Pity Miss Hodges is too old, or she would have done. Do you want to wash or wipe?"

They quite enjoyed getting down to it for even washing up is not so bad at someone else's sink. Everything was shining when they had finished.

" I'd love to give those curtains a good wash some time," Miranda declared.

" Come on," urged her sister. " Let's get our own ready first before we take on anything else. I want to see the lino cuts."

They left their appreciative neighbour, who promised to tackle the next washing-up before it got out of hand, and went back over the wall again. Miss Hodges was just going out, but she said that she would like to see how they had got on.

Miranda's effort was quite a pleasing conventional design about four inches square, based on leaf forms.

" Um-m-m, I like that ! " Miss Hodges remarked, to Julian's surprise. He himself produced a little steamer with smoke puffing out of the funnel. It was boldly designed, and was ploughing through the waves which rippled round her. " I thought it would remind Dad of his trip," he said.

" It's quite good. You see, you often get better results with a simple design. Now for Verna's."

" I did something nautical too," she said, " Although I didn't know that Julian was going to ! " It was a light-house on a rock, with rays of light flashing out. Miss Hodges also approved of this, and Verna glowed with satisfaction, for she had not found it easy.

Giles held his out slightly defiantly. " I thought it would be rather nice to do a picture of Mamie," he said. Mamie was bolt upright, and had almond-shaped eyes and rather a squint, which gave her a malevolent look.

"Oh dear," Miranda thought, "I don't want to hurt Giles's feelings, but fancy waking up in the morning to five hundred green Mamies! More like a nightmare."

"It's certainly original," Miss Hodges said cautiously. "It's the sort of design which can look very effective printed on a handkerchief."

"Couldn't you print one and give it to Dad for his birthday?" Julian suggested, seeing a way out. "You could buy a plain white handkerchief for two shillings." Giles ran his fingers through his chestnut hair. "That would be a good idea! He would know that no one else had a hanky just like it."

"That's right. Exclusive." The girls could not resist glancing at each other with looks which said "Saved!"

"I suggest," Miss Hodges said, "that you use this largest block for the bedspread, and both of these others —the steamer and the lighthouse—for the curtains. The two would go well together, and you could alternate them. I think you should add some waves to yours, Verna, dashing against the rocks."

They all thought this a good idea, and Giles did not mind in the least that his block was not to be used in Dad's room, since it was going to appear on an "exclusive handkerchief."

CHAPTER THIRTEEN

THE WORK PROGRESSES

THEY WERE itching to start. They found some old bits of sheeting to practise on, and Miss Hodges brought down some fat tubes of ink in two shades of green, which they bought from her. She showed them how to use the roller, and the mallet, making the thumping sound they recognised.

Miranda was the most successful, then Julian, so they decided that Miranda should do the bedspread, and Julian, most of the curtains, with Verna printing a few blocks so as to feel she had taken part.

They used the old kitchen table for the bedspread, and a large drawing-board on the floor for the curtains. Miss Hodges padded the surfaces, and showed them how to divide the bedspread into sections with tightly drawn string, and light markings. She watched Miranda print the first block, then left her to it.

Miranda worked slowly at first, stiff with nervousness, but gradually speeded up. After an hour she stood back to get the full effect, and felt really pleased.

" Hi ! You can come in now," she called.

Their " Oh's " and " Ah's " of surprise made her feel that the effort was worth her stiff back and aching fingers and wrist, so she decided to call it a day.

Julian decided that he would start the next morning before anyone was up. He wound the alarm and got down soon after six. He took the others up cups of tea for a treat, had some orange juice and biscuits, and got in an hour on the first curtain.

It was not easy to space out, as the blocks were smaller and further apart ; then he thought of tracing paper. He marked a large sheet into squares, then pricked through the intersections of the lines, finally marking the pin pricks with a tiny pencil mark.

A sleepy Verna appeared.

" It's smashing ! " she exclaimed. " Oh, I see—you've left the alternate spaces for my lighthouse."

" Yes. It'll be the darker green, and I didn't want to clean the inking slab each time."

" I'm dying to start."

" Don't spoil it, then."

" I'll wait till you get to the bottom where it doesn't show so much," she said, and went to get the milk from the back door. Mamie strolled in, ready for breakfast. She was just lifting one front paw delicately, to step on to the drawing board when Verna gave an agonised shriek which sent Mamie off looking very offended.

" Her paws were dirty ! " Verna cried. " You need eyes all round you when she's about ! "

They all decided that breakfast out of doors would be nice. Miranda said, " Let's go at the printing and finish it to-day. I want to cut a smaller block and print it in the empty squares in dark green."

" When am I going to have a look in ? " Giles inquired. " I haven't done anything yet."

" You might start by buying the handkerchief."

" Oh, of course ! " In two minutes he was off on his bicycle to the shops.

" Good thing it's cold meat to-day," Verna remarked. " So we needn't use the kitchen. Let's have salad, and oranges after it, so there won't be steam from cooking. You'd better start first, Miranda, because the bedspread is a long job."

It seemed to be their lucky day. Miranda was able to work steadily for an hour. Half-way through, Verna's friend Jane turned up with the latest pop records, so while she and Verna fell over each other's feet trying out the latest steps, Miranda hummed and tapped her feet.

She joined the girls when Giles was installed in the kitchen with Mamie curled up by his side to give him inspiration.

His handkerchief did not take him long, for he merely started at one corner, printed grey cats all round the edge, then continued in a kind of square spiral until he came to the middle. When he had finished he called the girls in to see and stood, his bright hair on end and his face quivering with excitement because he had printed Mamie's eyes in green from a tiny block. " Look at yourself, Mamie—look, my beautiful ! " he said proudly.

It really was effective, and although Giles had never once got a perfect print, they were evenly uneven, which odd as it may seem, is quite possible, and the slightly blurred effect was rather effective.

" That's jolly good ! " Verna declared. " Put it some-where to dry. I say, the green eyes look smashing ! I shouldn't leave it in the kitchen or Mamie may jump up to look at herself again."

After lunch Miranda cut her second block while Julian and Verna continued with the first curtain and started on the second. Verna printed her green .ighthouse a few times, but not in a complete row in case the slight difference between her printing and Julian's should be noticeable.

When Miss Hodges came in she seemed agreeably surprised at the results, for the four of them had had very little practice. She liked Miranda's second design and felt it would balance well with the larger one. " Don't rush it," she said. " Finish it to-morrow."

Julian and Verna decided to go and get on with theirs so as to finish it that evening, while Miranda hoped to complete hers the next day. " I think it had better go up in Dad's bedroom, on the floor," she said ; " we can't risk Mamie jumping up on it. I'll go and put down some newspaper."

The girls took the bedspread up, and carefully spread it out.

"There ! " Miranda said with justifiable pride, " although I says it as shouldn't, it does look dandy ! Make sure you close the door, Verna. We don't want our little four-footed friend strolling over it."

The next day, another "four-footed friend" was to affect them all, if they did but know it.

The next morning the girls were the ones to get up early. They worked together, one at the table and the other on the floor although it meant some waiting, and by the time the others came strolling down the printing was nearly finished.

" *Some* people," Julian began pointedly, " don't think to bring cups of tea up to other people who brought *them* up cups of tea. Naming no names."

" Oh dear ! we didn't notice the time ! Put the kettle on, will you ? I've only got two more prints to do. Give us five minutes, and we'll have all this cleared up. If a bite would stand between you and starvation, there's a nice crust in the bin which I was keeping for myself. As a mark of esteem I'll let you have it."

Back went everything after breakfast into Dad's bedroom, laid on the floor. They were dying to see what the curtains looked like hanging up, but they decided that they ought to get their handiwork "passed" by Miss Hodges before they counted it finished.

It was still ideal summer weather, almost too hot. When the phone rang and Nicky Weaver's voice was heard inquiring if they would like to go to the swimming baths, and back to the Weavers for lunch, they all cheered. That was just the thing for a hot day.

"No cooking for me to do!" Miranda said happily. "I couldn't think what to have to-day. We've eaten into the joint so much that with the scrap of lamb left, a shepherd's pie would be practically vegetarian."

"I should think the last thing a shepherd would want to eat in a pie would be lamb. Well, it's not our worry to-day, what to cook for lunch."

The bath was rather full when they got there, but after a time the numbers thinned out, and they were able to get some races. They had some practice at life-saving, and at one o'clock six ravenous people rode back to Weavers' Cottage.

Mrs. Weaver was at the sink, putting some onions into a saucepan as they came in. Verna hoped that that didn't mean half an hour's wait for lunch, and was relieved when Mrs. Weaver said that she was only dyeing some wool orange with onion skins. "It's for one of our 'olde worlde' customers, as we call them! The sort that like all the dyes to be vegetable, and not chemical. Now, you must all want your lunch. It's all ready."

Nicky and Julian went for a cycle ride after lunch, but the others said it was too hot, and read magazines in the Weavers' garden.

The two older girls were looking at hair styles.

"I'd love to go to a first-class hairdresser, and have my hair styled," Miranda said, looking enviously at the photographs in a glossy magazine.

"They'd probably want to chop a lot off—they always do," Jo Ann said. "A friend of Mummy's did, and she didn't recognise herself when she saw herself in the mirror afterwards."

"Gosh! but that might be an advantage! I'll have to see what Dad says."

"You can't *see* what a person says," Giles said dreamily. "You can only hear it. All you see is their mouth opening and shutting, like a goldfish. You can't *see* words, any more than you can *hear* the colour of anything."

"You can nearly hear the colour of your hair, when the sun's on it. It nearly stands up and screams. You go to sleep."

The six of them went back to the Harveys' house for tea. Mrs. Weaver gave them a tin of her shortbread, and they bought buns on the way back.

As Miranda took a large plate of sandwiches into the garden, a puppy of indeterminate breed trundled up the side way, looked around, then jumped playfully up at a butterfly.

"Oh, what a pet!" Verna cried. "I wonder where he belongs? He hasn't got a collar on. Come here, Boy, and shake hands." They threw a ball for him to run after, and he soon became friendly, although he was too lively round the tea things for their liking.

"This doughnut's got hardly any jam in it," Giles complained. "They need a good dollup."

"Go and get the pot of strawberry jam from the pantry, then. But don't forget to shut the pantry door, because of the flies." Giles went in, found the jam, then hearing a lot of laughter, dashed out into the garden to hear what the joke was. Amid laughter, they told him that Miranda had turned to pour out a cup of tea, and the next moment had found that her sandwich had disappeared. She had accused Julian of playing a trick on her, and while he was vigorously denying it, he had noticed that HIS bun was missing. He began to launch a counter-accusation when Verna caught sight of the puppy eating it with great satisfaction.

Tea was a prolonged affair. Seeing the puppy chasing about made them feel hot and no one felt like moving. About six o'clock the Weavers offered to help wash up. Their offer was refused, as Miranda said that they would get in each other's way, so the guests went off.

They carried in the tea things, and as Miranda went towards the pantry with the milk and sugar she called out: "You *didn't* shut the pantry door, Giles! I told you I didn't want flies round the food. They can't get through the wire mesh at the window, but that's no good if we leave—— " The next moment she stood aghast, then bent down over something on the floor.

"Oh heavens! Look at this—look at what's happened!"

The others crowded round her. Miranda held up the

wire stand which held the old grocery accounts and which used to hang from a hook on the inside of the pantry door. From it hung bits of tattered invoices, and chewed bits of an envelope, bits of which fluttered to the ground as she spoke . . . bits of chewed pound notes . . . their housekeeping money for the next three weeks.

CHAPTER FOURTEEN

DISASTER!

' THE PUPPY," said Julian quietly and his face was pale.

"Yes. But he couldn't have jumped up as far as the hook and knocked it off! Did you jog it off when you were in the pantry getting the jam, Giles?"

"Well, . . . I—I heard something f-f-fall as I came out!" Giles stammered. "I—I didn't stop to p-p-pick it up."

"Why ever didn't you be careful when the puppy was about?" Verna wailed. "We can't blame *him* for this."

"I . . . I——"

"Oh dear!" Miranda thought in dismay, even in her consternation, "is that stammering coming back again?" Giles had had a bout of it three years before, about the time he used to get nightmares and wake up screaming.

"Nobody would have thought of the puppy getting at it," she said more quietly. "You didn't realise——"

"It's my f-f-fault!" Giles said, his big eyes glittering with fright. "Y-you asked me if I h-had shut the door, and I didn't b-b-bother to make sure. I'll give all my p-pocket-money——"

Julian felt it was time he intervened.

"Look, Giles, don't get in a flap about it. We'll manage somehow! Nobody's going to starve! Nine times out of ten nothing would have happened, even if the puppy did go into the kitchen and find the pantry door open . . ."

Giles, looking up at him with big eyes, felt that there was something in having a big brother, in spite of their occasional bickerings.

"After all we've got the five pound note," Julian went on.

"But we w-wanted to *keep* it and g-give it back to Dad."

"He left it for emergencies," Miranda said reasonably. "And if this isn't an emergency, I don't know what is."

"Let's see—there was three weeks' housekeeping money there, wasn't there? That's twelve pounds——" Verna said, then wished she hadn't.

"Twelve pounds! Is it all chewed up?"

Miranda picked over the pieces. "Yes—all in bits. Oh well, we'll have to take down the note again. It can't be helped."

"Is there any money in the house-keeping purse?" Miranda fetched it and had a look. "Seven and fourpence halfpenny. The trouble is, we've all got such good appetites! And it's things like meat, and bacon and butter that use up the money."

"We'll just have to economise."

"But c-can we live on f-five pounds seven and fourpence, the four of us?"

"We'll jolly well have a try," Julian said, not feeling quite so optimistic as he sounded. "We can each give some of our pocket-money, can't we?" The others agreed immediately.

"Do you think we shall have to ask Aunt Eleanor for some money?" Verna asked.

"Not if we can possibly help it," was Miranda's decided reply.

She threw the remnants of chewed paper into the box which served as the kitchen waste basket, then they washed up in silence. There was a good radio programme on, and for an hour they felt cheered up. Verna and Giles went up to bed without any argument.

"Let's talk over things a bit. We can't let Giles feel too badly about it, poor kid! And Verna's only eleven—she shouldn't have to worry too much where the next meal is coming from."

"Let's count up how much we've got between us. There's the five pound note, then seven and fourpence halfpenny. How much pocket money is left?"

"Let's see—um-m . . ." After some totting up it came to one pound seventeen. "That's seven pounds four. Are there any bills to pay?"

"This week's milk. We'll just have to live on stodge that fills, Julian! Bread, and potatoes, and apples. They're not large, but they'll stew."

No one felt very cheerful next morning at breakfast. There was bacon in the pantry, but Miranda decided to keep it for lunch, so they had cereal, toast and marmalade. Verna stretched out for more toast, then she drew back, with a guilty expression on her face.

"Take it, Verna!" Miranda said sharply. "I won't have anyone feeling that they must go without. Tell them about the pocket-money, will you, Julian?"

"We want you to let Miranda and me use it, and we'll see if Dad can make it up to you when he comes back."

"I don't want m-mine back," Giles said quickly.

"Well, we'll see. Now shall we go over to Mr. Blake and cut down the canes that fruited this year? He's got

to take it easy." They thought this a good idea, so at ten
o'clock they went over.

"Don't say anything about our temporary financial
embarrassment," Julian murmured. "Shortage of money
to you, Giles."

Mr. Blake was in the garden, typing at a little table.

"Oh, hullo!" he greeted them. "Nice to have
company!" They told him why they had come.
"That'll be a great help," he said. "I can't do much
gardening—it gives me headaches. Just a moment, I'll get
some secateurs."

They put on old gloves to keep off the prickles.

"Don't cut down the new canes," Julian warned, "or
Mr. Blake won't get much fruit next year—I looked it
up."

They took turns to use the secateurs, Mr. Blake's and
their own, two cutting and two gathering up the old canes
to burn. They had made a nice clean sweep when there
was a tuneful whistle from the direction of the house.

"That's 'Come to the cookhouse door, boys'!"
Julian exclaimed. The whistle was followed by a shout of
"ELEVENSES!"

On the garden table was a large jug of orangeade, and
two big packets of biscuits. It was pleasant to relax on the
little lawn and discuss where they should burn the canes.
They would keep well away from fences, this time!

"I haven't forgotten about our outing," Mr. Blake
said suddenly. "And I wondered if you would like to go
to the circus. There's a big one over at Amblehurst this
week——"

"Oh, lovely!"

"Thanks awfully, Mr. Blake!"

" Super ! Oh, thank you very much, Mr. Blake ! "

" Then I'll get the tickets. Will any day this week do ? Good. And, by the way, could we drop the ' Mr. Blake ' ? It makes me feel like a schoolmaster with four of his pupils ! And although I may seem near middle-aged to some of you, I'm really not many years older ! "

" You're Simon, aren't you ? " Giles said gravely. " I like that name." And so it was Simon from then on.

When the orangeade was finished up, Simon looked at the girls with a comical expression.

" If any young lady should offer to wash up, the offer will be gratefully accepted," he said. " In fact, I'm dying for you to see the kitchen."

The washing-up this time was only a matter of five glasses and a jug, as they had eaten the biscuits from the packets. The kitchen did its owner great credit, and the girls told him so. There were no dirty dishes about, the sink had been scoured, and the table had an almost clean cloth on it.

They finished cutting down the canes, then stacked them up in a nice clear space. In ten minutes they were reduced to ash, ready to go on the garden. Simon went in to phone the box-office about the tickets, and came out to tell them that he could only get five seats together if they went the following night. " We'll have to pick up the tickets thirty minutes before it starts," he said, " but we can have a stroll before we go in. And what about having supper in Amblehurst afterwards ? There's a café opposite the circus grounds, and we'll be hungry by then."

They all thought that that would be lovely.

" You'd better have a word with Miss—what's her name ? Hodges, as we might not be back until getting on

for midnight, and she's just a bit responsible for you,
isn't she? Tell her it's nearly thirty miles ride. I think
we can all pile into my old car."

As they went back over the wall Giles remarked, "That
will save us one meal, won't it? I say, Miranda—I took
a biscuit every time Simon offered me one, even when I
had had enough, and I put them in my pocket for our tea.
Do you think it was quite honest?" Miranda said that
she didn't think that it mattered, but that it would be
better not to make a habit of it.

"Dad said send the sheets to the laundry, didn't he?"
Verna said suddenly. "But he didn't say we HAD to, so
we'd better do them ourselves. We could just put them
through the wringer, couldn't we, instead of ironing
them?"

"Oh, I'll give them a rub over."

"We'll do them after lunch then."

They brought in the washing a few hours later, just
ready for ironing, and were just going to start when they
heard a noisy little car draw up outside the house. Verna
had just gone upstairs with a "drip dry" skirt which was
ready to be put away, and looked out of a front window.

"It's Mrs. Bostock!" she called down. "She's coming
up the path."

Much as she liked Mrs. Bostock, for a moment Miranda's
heart sank. Had she come to say that she was fit enough
for work again? Perhaps she wanted to start to-morrow.
How could they tell her that they didn't want her, because
they could not pay her her wages! Oh, what a predica-
ment!

"Well, ducks, I just popped along to see you, now that
I am back," the genial voice began. "Or rather, 'popped'"

isn't in it, really, because I'm still ' dot and carry,' but Bert's got the afternoon off, and he ran me over in his old bone-shaker."

"Oh do come in, Mrs. Bostock! It *is* nice to see you again! How is your leg now?"

"Doing nicely, really, but I've got to go to the hospital regular for exercises—physical therapy, they call it. Laugh! you should see us! A lot of old crocks, we are. There's a neighbour of mine goes, broke her ankle, she did, and they have her twiddling her toes about, picking up marbles with her right-hand toes—or right foot toes, I should say, and passing them to the toes of her other foot. *And* tying bits of string with her toes. I tell 'em we'll all be ready to do turns on the telly before they've finished with us."

Miranda shepherded Mrs. Bostock into the kitchen for a cup of tea. The kettle soon boiled, and fortunately there were a few biscuits—including Giles's secret hoard —in the tin.

"Now, how have you been getting on without your Dad?" Mrs. Bostock asked, over a good strong " cuppa."

They gave her all the news which they felt could be told, including the ending of the feud.

"That's very nice, I'm sure," she replied, then cast a critical eye round the kitchen.

"Not bad at all! I noticed you'd done the porch, but it could do with a good scrub. I'm dying to get back to work, ducks—— " Miranda held her breath—"but doctor says not for a few weeks—— " Miranda breathed freely again.

"You get really fit first, Mrs. Bostock! We'll manage. You mustn't risk a set-back, you're too valuable for that! "

She felt rather a hypocrite, saying this, for she was more concerned about the family's affairs than about having Mrs. Bostock back.

"That's nice of you, love. Not like some ladies I've worked for—have you get up from your death-bed, if they wanted to give a dinner-party. But you're always most considerate."

Bert rang just then, so Mrs. Bostock picked up her stick and stumped off. Thank goodness they did not have to worry about her wages !

They told Miss Hodges about the circus directly she came in. She thought an outing would do them good, " I'll take the chance to go to the theatre with a friend who can't get to matinees," she said. " I promised your father I would not leave you alone in the house at night. I'll get a taxi from the station, and I should get back by a quarter to twelve. Will you ask Mr. Blake if that will be convenient ? I don't want you waiting on the doorstep—— "

Simon said that would be fine, and he would wait with them if they arrived back before Miss Hodges.

CHAPTER FIFTEEN

THE CIRCUS, SHAKESPEARE, AND MAMIE

" I wish they'd *come!* " Verna said for the fifth time.
" Where *have* they got to? " They had gone for a
cycle ride.

The boys dashed in at twenty past five. " We called in
at Nicky's and Mrs. Weaver asked us in to tea, but we
were late already, so she gave us a hunk of cake each."

" Well buck up, then! Change into your flannels, and
wash first! We'll have Simon hooting any moment
now."

Simon *did* sound the horn just as Julian came down
the stairs three at a time.

The ride was hilarious. They joked and teased each
other, and although Simon rightly said that he had to
keep his eye on the road and was not to be drawn into the
conversation, however intellectual, they could see that he
did not miss much. There was a twinkle in his eye and
his mouth was curved into a smile most of the time.

The circus was wonderful! Simon sat in the middle,
with Julian one side and Miranda the other. Miranda
clutched Verna's arm at particularly hair-raising turns,
and sometimes clutched at Simon, but he didn't seem to
mind. Verna bounced about or screwed herself up,
according to how she was feeling. Giles, wide-eyed,
seemed to be in a world of his own. Miranda hoped it
would not lead to nightmares. Julian took a scientific

interest in the apparatus used by the trapeze artists and trick riders, while Simon seemed to like the lot.

They had a meal in a café before the ride back, which was somewhat quieter than the outward journey, but just as cheerful.

They had had to wait for a table at the café, so it was ten to twelve before they got back. Miss Hodges did not seem to be in, for there was no light on. Then they heard voices in the porch.

" I'll come up with you," Simon said.

A policeman was bending over someone who was sitting on the porch seat.

" Good evening, sir " he said. " Do you know this lady ? "

" Oh—it's Miss Hodges ! " Verna exclaimed. Miss Hodges sat rubbing her head and looking dazed.

" The lady's had a fall," the policeman explained. " I should get her indoors."

They sat her down on the hall chair and Julian got her some water.

" As I came past," the policeman began, " I saw someone standing in the porch. Then she tried a front window, then she went round the back. It seemed suspicious, sir, so I followed. She tried the back door, then she began to creep down the garden. She went along that path, then she must have caught her foot in something, for she pitched forward and hit her head. I got her to the porch and rang several times but there was no answer, so I was waiting until she was sufficiently recovered for me to question her. If she lives here it's all right, sir, but she seemed in a real tizzy. All she could say was ' Shakespeare's left ear.' She must have been knocked silly, begging her pardon, sir. 'Shakespeare's left ear,' I ask you ! "

" She must have gone for a spare key we keep for emergencies," said Julian.

" So that was it ? It's not safe to put keys under a doormat, or in a shed. Burglars seem to smell 'em out."

" We'll be very careful in future," Miranda promised, giving the others a look which meant, don't start explaining about Shakespeare. It was too late for that.

Miss Hodges was recovering. She thanked the constable, who said it was all part of his job. Miranda made some tea and offered him a cup, but he said thank you, but he wouldn't stop.

Then they heard Miss Hodges' version.

" The taxi met my train," she said, " and I was just thinking how well everything had gone as I came up the path and opened my bag to get my key. I had come without it ! After I had always prided myself on never forgetting it ! But then—'Pride comes before a fall,' they say.

" I tried the windows and back door, then I remembered the spare key which you said was kept on the rockery in the left ear of Shakespeare's bust. When I fell I felt dazed for a few minutes, and couldn't collect my thoughts. What a mercy it was that you arrived just then ! That constable might have taken me down to the police station and charged me with trying to get into an empty house ! "

It was nearly one o'clock when they finally got to bed, and Verna was nearly asleep standing up. As the next day was Saturday Miss Hodges could stay in bed. Miranda said that she would take her up her breakfast, and said that the others could sleep on as long as they liked.

It was nearly ten when Julian and Verna came down, but Miranda had been up since nine, and Giles also. Miss Hodges was none the worse for her fall, except for a slight headache, but a cup of tea soon got rid of that.

Directly Giles had had breakfast, he announced that he was going to groom Mamie for the Pets Competition. " I'm going to bath her," he said. " Have you got any nice-smelling soap I can use, Miranda ? "

" Soap ? I've a little lavender soap that you can use. You'll find it in the bathroom, but you'll have to use the tin bath out in the garden. We don't want water splashed all over the kitchen."

A protesting Mamie was bathed with difficulty, dried with a towel and left to sun herself in the garden, while Giles went in search of something.

Half an hour later as Miranda was washing up, Verna came in inquiring " Whatever is that queer smell ? It's eucalyptus oil, isn't it ? Has anyone got a cold ? "

" It *is* eucalyptus oil ! Who's been using it ? "

When Mamie came in, the answer was evident. Her coat was plastered down and shiny, and she reeked of the oil.

" So *that's* what Giles has been up to ! " Miranda said in an exasperated voice. " *Look* at her ! You'd think the inhabitants of a whole village had colds in the head, by the smell of it ! Why did I buy a large-size bottle ! Giles !—come here."

When he came in they could see that even he had doubts as to the wisdom of his action.

" I wanted to make her coat glisten," he said in defence. " I looked in the bathroom cabinet to see if there was any brilliantine, but there wasn't, and there wasn't any in Dad's bedroom. But I saw a bottle of oil in the medicine chest, and I thought it would do."

" Well, if you leave it on that's the best way to spoil Mamie's chance of a prize. Some people can't bear the smell of eucalyptus oil. You are an idiot, Giles ! "

Giles went pink, partly at Miranda's scathing remarks, but mostly because he felt he had let Mamie down. He began to stammer again, Miranda noticed.

" I—I only did it to m-m-make her beautiful ! What can I do ? Will it r-rub off ? "

" No, you'll never get rid of the smell that way ! You'll have to bath her again—— "

" She hates being bathed ! And I d-did want her to get a prize ! "

Miranda felt sorry for Giles when she saw the look of tragedy in his eyes. He always felt things so deeply.

" Look—I'll help you bath her, and it needn't take more than a few minutes. We'll put some scent in the water. And . . . I know, I've got some hair-setting lotion you can put on afterwards. It makes your hair shine, so it may be as good as oil. It's in my dressing-table drawer."

Giles's face brightened. He ran upstairs and came down with a bottle marked : ' Blue Moonlight Setting Lotion.'

" Will it turn fur blue ? She'd look like a Persian, then."

" No, it won't. It's funny, isn't it ? And the green kind doesn't show any green once it's on, either."

A freshly bathed Mamie, looking disgusted at this drastic treatment, had the setting lotion poured over her and it was left to dry in the sun. Then Miranda flicked

Mamie's fur up with a soft brush, and then smoothed it down, leaving a very sleek and sophisticated looking cat. What with lavender soap, 'April Blossoms' scent and Blue Moonlight setting lotion, Mamie did not know herself and had a dazed expression not unlike the look on Miss Hodges' face the night before.

"She smells like a beauty parlour!" Miranda exclaimed. "I should keep her in the kitchen until you take her to the fête, in case she rolls on the dusty grass."

Giles went off to look for something large enough to carry Mamie in, so Verna took the chance to have a private word with her sister.

"Giles will be dreadfully disappointed if Mamie doesn't win a prize. Do you think I could possibly spend sixpence on a tin of salmon paste? If she doesn't win, it could be a consolation prize, and if by any chance she does, it would be something to celebrate with."

Miranda thought this a good idea, and Verna added it to the shopping list.

"You go down to the shops, will you, Verna?" her sister said. "And ask the butcher for a cheap cut. Tell him you don't know much about meat and you'd be glad of his advice. They rather like to be consulted, it's a bit flattering to them. We'll use the combined pocket-money to-day and we won't touch the five pound note until next week." Secretly Miranda disliked the idea of asking for cheap cuts, but she knew that it wouldn't worry Verna much.

There were no luxuries on the list, the food being of the 'stodge' variety—cheap and filling. Verna was soon back, and dumped the basket down on the kitchen table.

"I did rather well!" she exclaimed. "Mr. Dale was

very nice and he told me about the different joints. There's something called scrag end of neck of mutton. It sounds horrid, doesn't it, like a wizened old great grandfather of a sheep. But it's cheap. Then there's beef skirt, and he said that to be quite honest, it tastes like one, the way some people cook it, and it mustn't be hurried. That's fairly cheap too. Some of the most expensive cuts are fillet steak and rump steak. I got a good big bit of the scrag end, and he told me how to cook it."

"You'd better take it on, then. And do some apples, will you? I've got some ironing to do."

When the scrag end was on the table, smelling quite appetising with potatoes and two carrots and an onion which Verna had found in the vegetable rack, Giles came in wreathed in smiles.

"Simon will take us to the fête in his car. That will be a much more convenient way of taking Mamie than in a basket. I think that would have shattered her nerves. I believe she suffers from claustrophobia—she never likes being shut in a cupboard by accident."

"Giles, did you ask him to take us?"

"No. Not *ask*."

"That means you kind of hinted."

"I only went over and asked him what time he thought of going, and he said, oh, any old time, and I said did he think that as Mamie suffers from claustrophobia, would it spoil her chances of winning a prize if I took her in a covered basket? And he said well perhaps it would, and if it would be any help he would run us there."

"Giles, you are the limit! He must have known what you were driving at."

"I didn't exactly ask," Giles said in a pained voice.

" He needn't have offered." No, but one look at your expression, and he was lost, Miranda thought.

At half past two the long-suffering Mamie was carried tenderly into Simon's old car, and they set off for the big meadow behind the church. The Pets Entry was to be early on, so that those animals which were not in cages, or which could not be let loose, could be taken home directly afterwards, and the owners could return to spend their money at the stalls.

Soon after the fête had been opened, a voice over the loudspeaker asked all those who had entered pets for the competition to go to the big tent. Giles had filled up his form and paid his shilling entrance fee the previous week. He lined up with boys and girls and a few adults.

It was quite an informal affair. A little collection of judges sat at one end of the tent, and all the pets were brought forward for inspection. If they could do any tricks, they were allowed to perform.

There were dogs and puppies; cats and kittens; hamsters, white mice, goldfish and rabbits. They all looked smart as new paint and the judges were finding it difficult to choose prize-winners.

When Mamie's time came to do her stuff, Giles carried her over to the judges, and put her down. She looked quite aristocratic as she coolly looked the judges over, then turned away with an elaborate yawn. The judges had to laugh. " She looks as if she might have sailed down the Nile with the Queen of Sheba," one of them said.

After all the animals had been seen, the judges called for six of them to be brought up again. There were two puppies, a rabbit, a kitten, a hamster, and—Mamie.

Giles was glad that the others were doing their duty

at the entertainment booths, for he felt anxious. Suppose Mamie didn't win a prize ! He would hate having to tell the others.

The puppies were most appealing, stumbling about on absurd little legs ; the rabbit's fur was surely the silkiest ever ! Again Giles brought Mamie up to the judges, and put her down on the ground.

She looked round about her, then strolled over towards a few boxes which were lying over by the side of the tent. She poised herself ready to spring up on one box marked : MARGARINE, and at the last instant drew back, and with a spring of incredible grace landed on the next box, which was labelled : BEST ENGLISH FARMHOUSE BUTTER.

A ripple of laughter went round the tent, and someone said, " She won't be put off by imitations ! " and another, " ' It was the *best* butter ! ' "

There was a moment's discussion, and then the prize for the pet with the most appeal was awarded to Binkie, one of the puppies. The one for the pet with the most personality went to—MAMIE !

Giles went up to receive the prize : five shillings, and a tin of cat food for the winner. He was so proud and delighted that after thanking the judges he rushed off to tell the others. Although they were surprised, they felt it was not the time to spoil Giles's pleasure by being facetious, and they tried to hide it, for Giles seemed to think that it was the most natural thing in the world for Mamie to win over the others.

" I ought to be getting back," Simon said. " I could take her back for you, and put her in your garden. Or if you want to take her, I'll wait for you."

" Could you wait while I do my half hour helping to give out the hoops on the Hoop-la please ? "

Simon was a little surprised that Giles did not intend to come back, but Giles felt that as he could not spend any money there, he might as well stay at home. When the others came back later, Verna was rejoicing because she had risked sixpence in a lucky dip and had pulled out a one and threepenny tablet of soap. The others had spent a few pence each, but they also wanted to avoid being involved in raffle tickets, and such like.

" Here's an extra prize for Mamie from the family," Verna said, producing the salmon paste. " She's done you proud." Giles was quite touched by this, as he was used to the family's remarks about his darling, and he was most polite to them all for the rest of the day. Before he went to bed he went to Miranda and held out the five shillings.

" Mamie wants you to take this," he said simply.

" Oh Giles ! It's a shame to take the prize money ! I know you wanted to put it towards a sleeping basket for Mamie ! "

" She wants to help. She's one of the family."

" We'll borrow it, then. When Dad comes home you can have it back !

CHAPTER SIXTEEN

DEFEAT, AND A RAY OF HOPE

THERE WAS a letter from Dad on Monday telling them that he would be home in about three weeks.

"Your letters made me feel that home wasn't so far away," he wrote. "The business side has been quite a success. When things seem touch and go, I bring out the family snaps, and that usually does the trick. But whether it is because they think I must be respectable, having such a family background, or whether it is in the nature of a consolation prize, I wouldn't know!"

That day, every tin, bottle or packet seemed to be nearly empty. Verna burnt the potatoes, so Giles was sent out for tomatoes to go with the lettuce; Verna washed her hair with toilet soap, and it looked awful; Miranda took in a parcel for Miss Hodges, with six and sixpence to pay, and then she looked in the house-keeping purse and knew that they had had it.

"Julian, I'm going to send Verna down to the butcher's," she called. "Come and look at the state of the exchequer."

Julian looked. "Oh well, we did our best."

Miranda wrote out a shopping list and called Verna. "I'm afraid the note will have to go," she said. "We've got to eat!"

"Oh, what a PITY!" Verna exclaimed. "Well, here goes."

She came back with another 'cheap cut' from the

butcher's, and also a big lump of dripping which, he said, was awfully good for toast, and cheaper than butter. Then at the baker's she had got a day-old loaf, and therefore cheaper. The grocer produced a generous pound of bacon bits—really for flavouring stews, but which contained quite a lot of pieces which would fry for breakfast. Verna was almost jubilant as she handed over the change.

Giles was lying under one of the apple trees trying to think of a way of earning some money. Suddenly he thought of the fabric printing—perhaps he could print some more handkerchiefs and sell them . . . He would have to get orders first, because of buying the handkerchiefs. If he could sell a two shilling handkerchief for three shillings, that wouldn't be bad . . .

Giles wandered into the house and went up for the handkerchief he had printed for Dad. " Who shall I try first ? " he wondered. Oh—Simon! He had thought Dad's bedroom looked awfully nice, and had told them that if he ever wanted some curtains printed, he would know where to go! Perhaps Simon had friends with birthdays coming along.

Simon was working at the little garden table. He greeted Giles cheerfully, threw him a toffee, and said that he could not leave his work for a few minutes. When he had finished he threw down his papers and inquired, " Well, spent your prize money yet ? Have you bought Mamie a mink rug ? "

" Not mink, milk ! The money went towards the milk bill. Oh dear—— " He remembered that this was to have been kept in the family.

" I say, old chap ! I didn't mean to be nosey—— "

Giles felt that, since he had said so much, he had better explain. Simon seemed one of them by now. Surely it wouldn't matter?

Simon listened in silence, and then said gravely, "Thank you for letting me into your confidence. Did any of you think of asking your friends to come to the rescue?"

"No—Julian and Miranda said that families should cope with that sort of thing themselves, if they could. I wasn't supposed to tell you, but I'm glad I did. It's beastly knowing that it's your fault in a way, even if the others *are* nice about it."

"Did the puppy chew the notes all up?"

"There were only bits left. Not one whole one."

"You threw them away, I suppose?"

"They went into the trash bin, I think. It's kept in the kitchen, and Mrs. Bostock used to empty it each week. But someone always started moaning that a coupon or something had been thrown away, and they'd go scratching over the dustbin. So Mrs. Bostock empties it now and then, but she warns us beforehand. Miranda does that now."

"Could I look at the remains of the notes?"

Giles stared. "Yes, if you like. But they are just pulp."

"Look, don't tell the others, old chap," Simon said. "In case it doesn't come to anything. Could you bring the box, or whatever it is, over here?"

Giles thought he could. He nipped over the wall and saw that nobody was about, then carried it down the garden. Simon leaned over the wall and hauled it up, then they took it down to the little lawn.

Soon the contents of the big box were tipped out. There

were old envelopes and paper bags, one sock of Verna's, some old knitting wool, and the pliers which Julian had been searching for.

Simon quickly discarded anything that could not be what they were looking for. Soon Giles pounced on something, and held up some bits of paper. After more sorting, everything that had been part of a pound note seemed to have been gathered up.

" I want those bits," Simon said. " Let's see—what's the time ? Ten to four . . . it'll have to wait until to-morrow."

" What are you going to do ? " Giles was feeling bewildered. What could Simon do ? Giles looked at the bits of chewed paper spread out on the grass. There was not even a quarter of each note left.

" You wait and see, because I'm not sure yet. I'll tell you to-morrow if it comes to anything."

They put all the trash back, except the sock, pliers and other articles which had obviously gone astray. They carried the box back to the wall and Giles got it back into the kitchen without being seen. Then he remembered the box with the handkerchief inside which he had left in the other garden. He ran back for it and found it down by the garden seat. Simon had gone into the house, and Giles did not feel like asking him about buying handkerchiefs. He could not see any sense in what Simon was doing yet Giles felt curiously comforted.

It was raining when they woke the next morning, but soft gentle rain which was needed for the gardens, which were getting parched. Miranda had watered the lettuce, and radishes the night before and this, she declared always brought on the rain soon after.

Nicky rang up after breakfast to tell Julian that he had bought some balsa wood and was going to make more models, and would Julian like to come over? Oh, and if Giles liked to come too, he could have some bits of wood and work on his own. His mother said that they could stay for lunch and tea. Jo Ann wasn't about, as she had been asked over to a friend's house.

Soon after this, the telephone rang again. Bryony Drew, a girl in Miranda's form, phoned to say that as it was wet she had had an urge to dressmake, and she had asked Jo Ann Weaver over. Bryony's mother couldn't resist buying remnants at sales, her daughter said, and had a drawer-full. She would let them each have a piece for a blouse or a cotton skirt, if they would like it. Her mother was going out, and so they could have the gramophone on all the time, and when they were hungry they would have a fry-up. Could both the girls come?"

"Could we?" Miranda exclaimed. Two free meals for everybody! It is awful, I can't think of anything except in terms of money. I hope the family crisis won't leave a permanent defect on my character, she thought.

They all set off about ten o'clock on their bicycles. Bryony lived three miles farther on than the Weaver's turning, but they wore macks and the girls put on head scarves, so the rain did not matter.

They had to pass Bay Tree Cottage, and as they reached Simon's gate he was coming out his front door. They waved and shouted to him and he called back, but they did not hear what he said.

It rained all the morning, in showers, in spite of the " rain before seven " saying, but the Harveys did not mind and were not even aware of it.

Julian and Nicky worked in the Weavers' large tool shed—a wonderful place to be in if you were keen on tools, for there was every possible kind there, including a power tool which the two elder boys were allowed to use—" Entirely at our own risk," Nicky said. They worked for some hours on a large model aeroplane, while Giles made a whole flotilla of tiny ships.

The dressmaking session passed off equally well. To the music of the latest pop singer, the four girls measured, cut, fitted and argued, machined and unpicked again. They put on their favourite disc six times, and about two o'clock, realising they were hungry, fried up bacon, mushrooms, potatoes and tomatoes, finishing up with tinned fruit and coffee.

They all got back about seven. " We've had a gorgeous time," Verna said. " We're going to finish the things to-morrow. Mrs. Drew says she thinks she'll go up to town for the day."

They were all listening to a radio programme when there was a ring at the front door. It was Simon.

"You could have come up the garden way," Verna said. " We go that way to YOU."

" Yes, I thought of that. But what is your father going to say when he comes home, if he sees me getting over your wall and strolling up your garden ? "

" Oh, we'll tell him," Verna said comfortably.

" I think I'd better call on him first. But this is what I've come about now," and he held out something which made them all sit up. It was a thin wad of very new one pound notes.

" Twelve pounds," he said quietly. " It's yours."

Three of them were so mystified that they could only

gape. Giles was in a whirl. How could Simon have turned those chewed-up notes into perfectly new ones ? Even conjurers didn't really . . . And then conversation broke out, after a stunned silence.

" But—but it *can't* be ours ! "

" Our twelve pounds were in bits, and we threw them away."

" You're not trying to be kind to us, are you ? Because we couldn't possibly accept."

" How did you know we were twelve pounds short ? "

" I told him," Giles said, before he could wonder whether he would get a scolding. " It sort of came out."

" Just in conversation," Simon said. " And it's a good thing it did really. You see, when I heard that there were some bits of the notes left, and that they had been thrown into the trash bin, as Giles said, I wondered if by any chance the numbers had not been destroyed. You see, if Bank of England notes are torn up or accidentally burnt, but the bit bearing the printed numbers and letters (the serial numbers they are called), still remain, the bank will give you the money. Then they cancel the notes at head-quarters. It's the serial numbers and letters that count."

Everybody began talking again.

" Why—I never knew that ! "

" However did you find the bits ? "

" Does that really all belong to us ? "

Simon glanced round at them. Miranda looked as if a great weight had been lifted off her shoulders. Julian was muttering " I just can't take it in ! " Giles had gone quite white with excitement. Verna, pink with happiness, flung her arms round Simon and called him an angel. " And to think that I've had my mind filled with scrag end and skirt!" Simon looked mystified for he had never heard of them.

"Tell us what happened, Simon," Miranda asked.

"Well, it was too late to go to the bank yesterday, after Giles had told me, so I went down this morning. That was when you passed. I saw my bank manager, and showed him the pieces. By wonderful luck, the puppy had bitten through the envelope and eaten through the middle of the notes, rather as you might take some bites of, say, a dozen of those thin wafer biscuits you have with ice cream, and then threw away the ends. We managed to find the serial numbers of the twelve notes, and the bank manager said that he would do the rest."

Giles spoke for the first time. "It's like waking up from a bad dream," he said. "Thank you very much, Simon." Now that the others had taken it in, they added their thanks to those of Giles.

"I wish— " began Miranda.

"You wish what?"

"Well . . . of course we can put five of those notes behind the picture of Saint Christopher—did Giles tell you about that?—but I do wish we could have put back the five pound note! It sounds silly, I'm sure, but I would have liked it to be still there when Dad came back. Of course it doesn't matter, really," Miranda felt that what she had said was not very tactful, like telling someone that you would rather have a pink umbrella when they had given you a blue one. "I'm terribly grateful to you," she added, but Simon seemed to understand.

"Do you know where you changed it?" he asked . . . The butcher's? Well, if he's banked it, or paid it out, there's not much we can do. But he may go to the bank on

Saturdays, so he may still have it. He can't have given it out in change ! Suppose one of you goes down to his shop when it opens. Half past eight, isn't it ? The bank opens at nine, so you might be lucky."

It was decided that Julian and Verna should take five of the pound notes to the butcher's and try their luck.

They got there just as the shop was opening, at half past eight. Mr. Dale was laying out joints on a marble slab, and greeted them cheerfully.

" Good morning   And it IS a good morning to-day, isn't it ? And what can I do for you, Miss ? I've got some nice economical cuts—— "

" Thank you, but first we want to ask you if you have still got the five pound note I changed the other day, Tuesday, it was, for the scrag end. You see, we want it back for a special reason. We've brought five one pound notes in exchange."

" Let me see—I'll look in the till, but Tuesday, I doubt it, what with paying out wages, and that . . . no, I'm afraid there's only this one, and I know Mrs. Watson paid for her shoulder of lamb with it, just before we shut yesterday . . . But you can have this one, if it will be of any use."

" No, I'm sorry, but we especially want the one I brought. For—for sentimental reasons, as you might say."

" Oh, for sentimental reasons." Mr. Dale looked at her gravely.

" I suppose you wouldn't happen to know what you did with it ? " Julian asked, as a forlorn hope.

" Let me see : Tuesday, you said it was ? . . . I nipped over to the newsagent's to pay the paper bill for the month, and I believe I gave the girl a five pound note.

Your best bid is to try there." They thanked him and went down the road to Curwood's. They knew Mr. Curwood well, and felt that he would not ask a lot of questions, and think them peculiar.

Mr. Curwood was very helpful. " Anything I can do to oblige! My wife is on the way to the bank now—if the note wasn't paid out, it will be in with the money she is paying in. If you run you can catch her up. Ask her to pop back here before she goes to the bank."

They dashed up the road and caught Mrs. Curwood just before she reached the bank. Julian was out of breath so he touched her on the arm. She turned a frightened face towards him.

" My! You gave me a scare! I thought it might be someone with a cosh, ready to snatch my bag! You're the Harvey children, aren't you? "

In a few minutes they were back at the shop. As Mrs. Curwood opened her bag she asked, " There are several five pound notes here. How will you know yours? "

" We've looked at it a number of times, and the number is indelibly printed on my mind," Verna said.

" I took the number when my father gave it to us," Julian said.

The next moment there was a whoop from Verna, and a whistle of satisfaction from her brother. There, on Mr. Curwood's counter, was the note which they had thought was gone for ever.

Julian brought out the pound notes from his pocket.

" Thanks awfully for bothering over it for us! And thank you very much for coming back, Mrs. Curwood. I'm afraid it has delayed you. But perhaps we can do some shopping, or something, for you, some time."

The good lady said that it was quite all right, and she was pleased to help, if that particular note was what they wanted so badly.

" We did really ! " Verna said earnestly. " It was for sentimental reasons."

Mr. Curwood and his wife watched the two Harveys jump on to their bicycles and ride away furiously. Then they looked at each other, puzzled. " Well, I dunno," the wife said. " It takes all sorts to make a world."

They asked Simon over to see the ceremonial putting back of the Note. As Julian fished out the roll of sellotape for the second time, he felt that all their effort had been worth it.

" Only about ten more days, Saint Christopher," Miranda said. " *Please* don't let it out of your sight."

CHAPTER SEVENTEEN

THE HARVEYS TOGETHER AGAIN

IT WAS a day of rejoicing ; the girls went off to Bryony's, where they and Jo Ann spent the morning happily refitting, unpicking, binding, putting on press studs and zips, and arguing, with the radiogram going at full blast all the time.

The boys were happy each in his own way. Julian went off to see how his two friends were getting on with their boat, and Giles went down to the public library and roamed round for an hour, then came back and read in the garden, stretched out under one of the apple trees.

The girls arrived back just before one o'clock, so lunch was a scratched meal. Miranda had said gaily, coming along, " We'll take in a tin of stewed steak to heat up, and have a tin of fruit salad afterwards, with cream ! No more stewed apples for a little while."

" No we can't," Verna said calmly. " Dad said : only one tin to be opened a day. You know he was afraid we wouldn't get enough vitamins and things."

" So he did ! I'd forgotten that. All right—sausages, then."

They put aside thoughts of cheap cuts, and economising, for the next day or two, but before long it was time to think about plans for welcoming Dad back.

" I want to make him a cake," said Giles, whose head had been slightly turned by the success of the one he had made for Miss Hodges.

" I should make a plain one this time, not a mosaic,"
Miranda said, with a suspicion of a twinkle in her eye.
" You could ice ' Welcome Home ' on it."

It was very pleasant for them all to be able to draw their
pocket-money again, and for Giles to have his prize
money back. He had his eye on a fireside basket for
Mamie, and it would not be long before he could buy it.

As the day of their father's return drew nearer there was
a skirmish of activity. Although Dad was not very
observant about such things as a little dust more or less,
the girls turned out the house right through. The window-
cleaner came just at the right time, the day Miranda took
a load of sheets and heavy things to the laundry.

Then the letter came, saying that Dad would be back on
the following Saturday, making it just under the six weeks
since he went away.

" I'm going to do a ' Welcome ' banner," Julian
announced. " We'll put it up over the porch." It took
him some hours, but it looked very nice when it was done.
It said :

WELCOME HOME DAD !
THE BEST GUY
IN THE
OLD AND NEW WORLDS !

And there was a large map of America and Canada on one
side, and one of England on the other.

On the Friday, the girls got Dad's bedroom ready, with
a bowl of flowers on his bedside table, just to compete with
those American hotel bedrooms, Miranda said.

Giles was busy with his cake, and turned everybody out
out of the kitchen until he had finished. It looked very
successful, but Miranda privately decided to get a bought

one, just in case. She told Giles that she wanted to have plenty to eat for tea, in case Dad was hungry after his journey.

The next day came at last. Dad was expected home in the afternoon, so the girls decided to have tea directly he arrived and then dinner in the evening, instead of supper, to celebrate. Midday lunch was a scrappy affair, everybody being too busy and excited to stop for much, then the girls went shopping, for a chicken among other things. Mrs. Bostock had been consulted as to the cooking, and she had indeed offered to come and cook it for them, but the four Harveys felt that it had to be their day.

In the early afternoon the phone rang, and Dad's dear familiar voice could be heard, as clearly as if he were in the room with them. He told them that he was not sure which train he could catch, so they were not to meet any trains, and he would take a taxi.

The table was laid and made gay with flowers ; the banner was nailed up, and they all got into clean dresses, and shorts and shirts. Even their shoes had been cleaned by Julian, when he had had a few minutes to spare.

Giles stationed himself on the landing window-sill on the look out, and suddenly he shouted : " Here's the taxi ! " and bounded down the stairs. The next moment, everyone was at the gate. Out jumped Dad, and had a job to pay the driver, who stood grinning by, and then in the general confusion carried the luggage up to the porch.

Miranda hugged her father, and then felt that nothing could go wrong now. She was soon hustled away by the others, while Dad tried to look at them all at once.

When they got into the house, Dad was almost carried up to his bedroom. He stood in the doorway, speechless.

" We did it, Dad ! " Giles exclaimed, and then each one tried to tell their father how it had all come about. He could hardly believe that the curtains and bedspread was their handiwork.

" It's simply *beautiful !* " he declared. " When I wake up here I shall think that I must be on the *Queen Mary*, " and he couldn't understand what the burst of laughter was for.

He promised not to be more than five minutes getting ready for tea. When they were all sitting down he said, " Now I can really look at you all ! Now, tell me how you got on."

They told him some, but said that he would have to have it in bits, as they were *dying* to hear what he had been doing. Between cups of tea—the best he had had for six weeks, he said—and sandwiches and Giles's cake, which was highly praised, he told them what he had been doing. At the end of the meal he said, " Heavens ! what kind of a father am I ? You were all much too polite to mention it, but I've got something for each of you."

There was a necklace of many strands of beautiful coloured beads, the loveliest she had ever seen, and little ear-rings to match, for Miranda. Verna got a lovely bracelet with a dozen exciting little charms hanging from it. For Julian, there was a book on the industries of America, with colour photographs, and for Giles, a set of model racing cars. Besides these, there were " extras " from what Dad called " his rich American and Canadian friends," who, with their usual generosity, had sent nylons and jumpers for the girls, and microscopes and books for the boys. Mr. Harvey had not forgotten Miss Hodges, and had brought her a book of colour photographs.

"Dad, you seem to know *just* what people like!" Miranda exclaimed, looking at herself in the mirror.

"I know what *I* like," he replied, "Two daughters and two sons, and the dandiest ones you could find anywhere! Now I want to look at the 'Welcome' poster again."

This was duly admired, and then, as they came into the hall again Miranda said, "Look, Dad, we didn't have to use it," and she took down the picture of Saint Christopher and turned it over.

Dad looked at the five pound note, then at all of them.

"I needn't have worried about you," he said.

During dinner, they told him the history of the past six weeks. When they told him about Simon, and how he had been transformed from "Mr. Blake," their father said, "That's one of the nicest things you could tell me. I hated feeling that we were not on friendly terms with a neighbour."

"Can you invite him round, Dad?" Verna asked. "I think he's rather shy of meeting you."

The next day Dad showed them a letter for their approval. It ran:

"Dear Mr. Blake,

My children seemed to have managed, not only to run the household while I was away, but also to help end an unfortunate feud. I hope I may be allowed to enter into the friendship which has sprung up, and I shall be very glad if you will come over to smoke the pipe of peace—or you may prefer an American cork-tipped—this evening. Verna will be happy to bring your reply.

Yours,
Robert Harvey."

Simon came willingly, and over cigarettes and coffee, and orangeade and cake for the others, any awkwardness soon disappeared, and " Mr. Blake " became Simon to the whole family.

After he had gone, the united Harveys sat in the sitting-room with the french windows open, looking into the shabby garden, strangely transformed in the dusk into a place of beauty. Summer scents drifted in, and night moths flittered.

" Well, you must have had a busy time," Dad said, " what with one thing and another."

" Yes," Julian said. " There was no time for us to get bored. Some of the things had to be dealt with at once. Like getting in the raspberry harvest. That couldn't be put off."

" And there was another harvest you gathered in, too, during those weeks," Dad said quietly. They all looked at him in surprise.

" You held out the olive branch of peace, and you gathered in a harvest of friendship between neighbours. You'll do, all of you." And Miranda, looking at her father, knew what he meant.

THE END